Bonne Route
Stories

route 19

First published by Route
PO Box 167, Pontefract, WF8 4WW
info@route-online.com
www.route-online.com

ISBN: 978-1-901927-34-4
ISBN(10): 1-901927-34-2

Editor:
Ian Daley

Editorial support:
Anthony Cropper, Isabel Galán, Susana Galán,
Roger Green, Manuel Lafuente, Michael Lyng, Tony Maguire,
Oliver Mantell, Susan Tranter and Julie Weiss.

Cover design
Andy Campbell
www.dreamingmethods.com

Printed by CPI Bookmarque, Croydon

A catalogue for this book is available from the British Library

Route is an imprint of ID Publishing
www.id-publishing.com

This book was possible thanks to support from
Arts Council England

Stories

Rising Laughter
Dave Pescod

He's snoring again. It's worse since they changed his medication. I can't sleep and I can hear the neighbours talking in bed, through the wall. I can't hear the exact words, only the pattern. It undulates fast and slow, and ends with a pause when she laughs. It gets louder and he joins in. They'll wet themselves if they keep laughing like that. I get up and go to the kitchen and I can't help smiling at the strange sound of their infectious laughter.

It's been ages since Roy left the flat to brave the world, and even longer since we had a laugh. He's lost somewhere in his body, helpless in a dark place, just like his dad. But I don't want to give up trying. Those bloody pills aren't the answer.

He took me dancing when I was sixteen, and I couldn't see any sign of it. He'd laugh like anyone else, chortle and shake, become possessed as good as anyone. He could tell a good story, that's one of the things that attracted me to him. I'd watch him pace himself, embroider the plot, revel in the tale, then deliver the punchline. He'd glow and smile. I was proud of him.

They're still chuckling next door, like their teeth are scratching the wallpaper, taunting me. They can't leave it alone. I hear the door, he's off to work. There's a snigger through the kitchen window as he walks along the balcony. It must have been a good one.

I take Roy his breakfast. He doesn't say anything, just sits there po-faced as I pull the curtains to let the grey light in. I leave him staring into space. I could never tell jokes — too embarrassing. I'd forget the story and start giggling, turn bright red, and look for a hole to crawl into. I like most jokes, but there's a lot I don't understand. It's not that I don't understand the joke but I don't see what's funny. Sometimes they're just hurtful, like racist jokes or nasty ones about sexual perversion. But a good joke's like a piece of timeless magic. I can't remember jokes but I know exactly where it was I heard them, the colour of the wallpaper, a mole on the face of the person who told it, the way someone fell about laughing, gasping for air.

I wash up the breakfast things and water the daffodil bulbs on the windowsill.

The next night I'm out on the balcony having a cigarette. He won't let me smoke in the flat, not since the doctor made him give up. Three flats along I can hear them laughing, they're in hysterics. It's like a virus is breaking out. They close their window to muffle the laughter. I smile and nearly drop my ciggie down four floors, but I'm curious. What can be so funny?

I go in and sneak into bed beside him, he grunts and rolls over away from me. When we first met, I couldn't wait to sleep with him, to share his bed. I would have given anything, and it was worth it. He was a good lover, passionate and thoughtful. But, now it doesn't take much for me to creep out and curl up on the settee with some old film on the telly. He doesn't like me doing it, he likes me there, right next to him breathing the same air.

I've seen this film before, it's a western. When I turn it off I can hear chuckling in the distance, making its way along the corridors and down the stairwells, like bad plumbing. Or am I just imagining it? I can't tell but I fall asleep listening out for more. I'm a child again and Dad is telling me a story, it's sending me to sleep, safe and secure. I sleep for what seems a year, or was it five minutes? Soft laughter from somewhere in the block wakes me.

I get up, dress and go out to fetch his prescription. I bump into the next-door neighbour, Joyce, on the staircase. We exchange greetings, and I pluck up the courage to ask her.

'You were having a good laugh the other night.'

'Don't,' Joyce says slapping my arm, her eyes rolling behind the peroxide fringe. 'Bert came back from work with a cracker, best joke I've heard in years.' I raise my eyebrows in expectation, and she takes a breath. She describes the situation richly, one I can identify with, as most people would. Years fall off her as she acts the part. She looks me in the eye and assures me, describing the scene, building a picture, a place with warm people. I nod in encouragement, fully understanding the character's predicament. She balances carefully on the metal stairs, nail varnish against galvanised steel. I concentrate hard in case I get the wrong end of the stick, listening for anything significant, something that might be twisted, turned round and used in the punchline. She gets closer, her breath is rancid, her eyes wide open. She pauses, then slowly lets the final words leave her yellowing teeth and smudged lipstick. She pushes me away, hard against the handrail laughing at her own joke. I laugh, slowly at first, enjoying the intimacy, our bodies sliding out of control. My stomach muscles complain at this new exercise and tears start to roll down my face. She looks worried, but then she's laughing at my contortions. We are rag dolls hanging on the balcony, falling into each other. Gradually we gain air and inflate, our spines become stiff.

'Mind you, I don't tell it as well as Bert,' she says.

I light a ciggie and offer her one. She lights it off mine, and then asks.

'What about you, have you got one?'

I wipe my eyes and shake my head. She takes a drag of the ciggie then scuttles off like a disappointed dealer. I quickly memorise the joke's form and punchline, thinking about its pace and content.

My father was a travelling salesman and kept a joke book. He said you have to sell yourself and the product follows. If they like you, they'll like the goods, and everyone likes a joke, so that was his way in. His joke book had all his clients entered alphabetically, with their preferences next to their name. Like (sh) for shit jokes more popular up north, (m-i-l) for mother-in-law jokes - widely popular, (sex) jokes - very popular in the midlands. There was even (ESI) an Englishman, Scotsman and Irishman category, as well as many more. In the different sections the punchline would be written carefully in his tiny handwriting. Before calling on a client he would quickly sift the book and choose a joke to smooth the sale. He carried the book for twenty-two years, and then on his last week of work, he left it in a telephone box in Brighton. Its cracked black leather next to the calling cards of Rita the meter maid and Simone of S&M delights.

That's all I wanted when he died, his joke book, to remember those funny nights by the fire when he would have us in stitches. Roy would copy him and steal some of his jokes. I didn't mind, I thought it was flattery and Roy told them well. But, I never dared tell jokes at home, that was what Dad did, and I wouldn't have dreamt of treading on his toes.

I put Roy's medication in the cupboard and make the tea. I wish he wouldn't watch so much daytime television, especially the news. It just makes him worse. The Middle East and the starving in Africa, what can he possibly do about them?

Again that night I hear laughter rippling though the block, at first it's the mechanical laughter of the TV, alongside hi-fis and barking dogs. But later it's more eccentric, people gasping for air while Roy's fast asleep snoring. I make some hot chocolate then go to the bathroom. I look in the mirror, and I swear if I look hard enough I can still see the girl that wooed Roy, she's still there hiding behind the wrinkles and chins.

I tease her out with some silly facial expressions. She is smiling at me. I remember the first lines of the joke, and say them quietly, keeping a straight face, with just a faint glint in my eye. I recall the gestures, the drama, as the joke unfolds towards the twist, and the pause. She is looking expectantly through the cracked mirror, I take a breath and deliver the punchline with immaculate timing. She laughs with me. I stifle the laughs. I must not wake him. I put on some make-up and lipstick, a dress rehearsal. She looks happy, we are one, confident and charming. I tell the joke again with aplomb, celebrating under the forty-watt bulb and half-tiled wall. Two years I've been decorating the bathroom, but the Tesco job doesn't leave me much time.

After I've made his breakfast I go outside for a ciggie to find courage. I'm on late shift today. Bert from next door rushes by late for work. I wash up first then take him tea by the telly. I tidy the room and disconnect the digital box, but he doesn't notice for a while, then I switch the damn thing off. I place a chair directly in front of him, he looks puzzled. I smooth the folds from my dress and push back my hair.

I just begin, I don't announce it or give a rambling introduction. His face is the colour of pale cardboard but I can see a glint somewhere in those Valium eyes. I'm enjoying it. He is curious, like watching a documentary on the history channel he can't understand. I'm very slow and deliberate, making sure he follows the important parts that may be destroyed and turned over with the twist. I stand up, more room for gesture and expression. He is impressed but not overcome. I catch a glimpse of Roy at twenty-four, carrying three pints from the bar with a fag in the corner of his mouth. There are tiny red lines in his cardboard face moving blood from that heart I love. I'm gaining, I know what's coming but I mustn't laugh. I pause, then like a full kiss on his dry lips, I deliver the punchline. I chuckle a bit, but not enough to steal the response. I stare into a young Roy's eyes and very slowly they sparkle like a distant shooting star. His face lifts and the corner of his lips turn up. His hands let go of the tarnished armchair and he shakes his head slowly, in disbelief. Then a sound like a depth charge rumbles through his stomach, up his throat and delivers a small but perfect chuckle. He turns to me, with a smile, as his grey face starts to redden.

'You told it well, love. Just like your old man.'

Later that week, as we're walking down the stairs, we pause to let Joyce by. She greets Roy as if she'd seen him yesterday, then winks at me, raising her nail-bitten thumb. She carries on up the stairs, and Roy turns and calls to her, 'We're off to feed the ducks.'

The Ecstatic Pessimist

Carla Gericke

The ice-tray has not been filled in weeks, so, for Number One, I write: 'Fill ice-tray'. I spin around once in my fully adjustable Aeron chair and when I return to my starting point, I grab the corner of my desk, stop, and write: 'No. 2: Try to brush teeth every day'. I tap the words on the yellow legal pad. The phrase sounds defeatist, so I cross out 'Try to' and with dark lead swirls, I capitalize the 'B' leaving the more affirmative: 'Brush teeth every day'.

Pleased, I snatch up my tumbler and settle back, the netted backrest gives beneath my weight. Two down, eight to go, I think and swill more room temperature whiskey. Tray filling. Teeth brushing. Sadie would be proud. Three years ago, when we started living together, she discovered my penchant for making lists and nicknamed me 'TP'.

'Like a fucking tent?' I'd asked.

'As in ten-point. My ten-point man.' She'd wriggled her eyebrows to indicate she meant on every scale. 'But for smarts, ostensibly,' she grinned, 'only a three.' She held up three fingers in the universal okay sign. When I flipped up my middle finger at her, she'd laughed and said, 'Well, since you insist, I'll make it a four.'

I shake my head with brain-bruising strength to stop

myself thinking about her. No use going there. White spots whirl in front of my eyes, as though my brain is a gigantic snow-globe and my thoughts are fat floating flakes. Good one, Jay: to snow-globe.

v. snow-globed, snow-globing, snow-globes.

1. To shake one's head vigorously until all thoughts melt away. 2. Best if executed while highly intoxicated.

I swirl my drink, watching the amber liquid spin. Snow-globed, shaken not stirred. I snort loudly. I take another sip and replace the glass inside the now permanent white ring on my desk – my built-in coaster – when I notice my wristwatch lying face down next to the laptop.

Must have ripped it off last week, or maybe it's been longer? I can vaguely recall spinning around the room in my office chair, feet off the floor, arms akimbo, like a rock star Rio Jesus Christ on wheels, singing: 'T-iiiii-m-e is *not* on my side.'

I push off again and bounce my body against the backrest as I spin. I loathe this chair. After eleven years, two mergers, eleven multi-million dollar deals, you'd think they might have given it to me as a parting gift, as part of my package. But no, they expected everyone to do their bit for Team Fuck-Up. If you wanted one of the Herman Miller Aeron chairs they'd acquired after deciding the Internet was the way to go – due South, apparently – then you had to buy the goddamn ergonomic wonder yourself.

For a while, the room blurs pleasantly – shelf, window, cabinet – but when the chair's momentum slows, my gaze returns to the wristwatch. Unable to resist time's pull, I reach out for it. Eleven-sixteen a.m.? I slam my feet down. The chair jerks to a halt. *Eleven-sixteen a.m.?* I sling the Rolex across the room. It lands in a pile of dirty boxers on the sofa, a laundry load I haven't done.

Now definitely in the mood for addressing issues head-on, for Number Three, I write: 'No drinking'. The words look stark, blunt and extreme, so I add, 'before –'. I pause. Before when? What's a decent time of day to start drinking? Prior to this wonderful hiatus, I never imbibed during the day unless a work function called for it. But now? Now, Jack and I are tight. James Jonathan Jordan and Jack. Or James Jonathan Jordan and J&B. Or Jameson, now there's a real namesake. And then there's Johnnie, José and Jim. Jay Jay Jay Jay. What comes after cubed? The Double-Trouble Jay. Jay Cubed Plus One. Jay Squared Times Two. Jay to the Power of Four. Four? Shall we say four o'clock is a respectable cocktail hour? Come now, tsk, tsk, Mr Jay Jay Jay Jay. In order for this list to succeed, we must set achievable short-term goals.

Noon it is.

I gaze at the whiskey. Forty-four minutes? No problem. But, wait. How will I know when it's exactly noon? In order to maximize the success of the New Me Plan and in order to accurately meet my carefully defined timeline, I'll need to retrieve the watch.

I scramble towards the sofa. Since I'm up, I decide to save myself another trip later so I snatch the J&B off the coffee table and tuck it under my arm. I grab the watch and as I turn back, an envelope addressed to 'Mr Jay Jordan and Miss Sadie Brown' catches my eye. A wedding invitation from Michelle and Elijah. We were supposed to be next. Michelle is Sadie's friend. Elijah's mine. We'd introduced them to each other, worrying at the time about whether they would end up hating us if things didn't work out. Yeah, right. Didn't work out for *them*, I mean. I head back to my desk, unscrewing the bottle top with my teeth as I walk.

'Has the invite arrived?' Sadie asked yesterday over the phone. No hello. It was the first time we'd spoken in two weeks.

'Hey babes, how ya doin'?'

'How are *you*?'

'Oh you know. Same-ohshame-oh.'

'Are you drunk?' The 'again' was unspoken but it hung there anyway.

'Me?'

She sighed. 'Who else? It's three in the afternoon.' She sighed again. I could almost feel the force of the air through the earpiece.

'Good question. My alter ego has some thoughts about that. Wanna talk to him?'

'TP.' Sigh. A grade three, at least. 'Have you checked the mail? Mich's –'

'But, of course, my darling.' I glanced at the pile of mail on the table, a good few weeks worth. 'In fact, I was just getting ready to call you.' We both knew it was a lie.

'Remember that time we went with Mich and Eli to

20

Stockholm and –' she started then stopped. When Sadie first left, she would do this all the time. Call and talk about the past. Places we'd been happy. People we'd been happy with. I guess she was trying to ground me. Make me believe we could go back to what we'd had before.

'When what?' I asked, happy to play along. I took a sip of whiskey and the glass accidentally tapped against the receiver.

'Never mind.' No sigh, just a small sad-mad sound, almost a whimper.

'When what? Come on, tell me, Sexy Sadie oooh how did you know...' I crooned. I was still building up to her favourite part when she hung up. Not being a quitter, I finished the song while the dial tone bleated in my ear.

Back at my desk, I prop up the watch so I can observe the minutes as they tick by. In the meanwhile, I top off my drink in anticipation of High Noon. Preparation and planning is key to any project, and I'm determined not to miss this launch date.

Ready, I focus back on the list. Then I glance back at the glass. Technically, today is the day for sorting out what is going to happen to the New Me in the future. I've already been drinking all morning, so it only seems sensible that I should wait until tomorrow to implement the new rule. My hand inches towards the glass, closing around it. I toast the ceiling and chug.

Wiping my lips, I glance around and Number Four comes easily. 'Call cleaning service'. The bathroom could certainly use a scrubbing, and God knows what's breeding in the carpets. I haven't been upstairs in a while, preferring to sleep on the sofa conveniently located in front of the TV. The last time I was up there was when Sadie came back to pack.

'Why are you doing this?' she said, the corner of her mouth curling in that way it did when she was trying hard not to cry.

'Doing what?'

'This –' her arms flailed, encircling the room, which, come to think of it, didn't look so hot, 'to yourself. To us.'

I snow-globe again, shaking my head like a wet dog straight out of the pool. When the orange polka dots subside, I write: 'Subsection 4(a): Deal with upstairs'. The way the subsection looks on the page is pleasing, it looks so organised and logical, and I decide to cram a few others into the space allotted for Number Four, careful not to cross over into Number Five's territory. It's imperative to not foul up the system. There's almost the entire alphabet of things to do around the house.

My brain's momentary relapse, my thoughts of Sadie, has not gone entirely unnoticed. Boxers are so comfortable, I think, tapping my erection against my stomach. The question is, Jay my man, whether we deal with this now, or later? My left hand decides to at least go say 'Hello' while the rest of us figure it out. My traitorous right hand seems compelled to pen Number Five: 'Quit masturbating so much'. I nod in approval at the generality of this statement. Unlike the rigid noon lift-off, this one has a viable, let's-work-with-the-situation-as-it-arises feel to it. Doable.

KABLAM!

The kitchen! I leap to my feet and race towards the kitchen, still clutching my penis in one hand. I skid to a halt at the door and survey the room. The microwave's door has blown open. An ungodly-coloured, thick, gooey substance covers an impressive portion of the counter and floor.

I shake my head in disgust. Cheese. Everywhere. Since my college days, I've set the microwave on full power for as long as it can go and then waited patiently for just the right moment to rescue whatever I was nuking from the microwave's rays. It's a true skill, one I've honed over many years. I am Microwave Man. I instinctually know the exact moment when food is perfectly cooked. I understand on a molecular level the precise length of time each dish needs to be nuked in order to get the best results. I can't believe I abandoned the mac.

The phone rings. I stroke my dick while I wait for the answering machine to pick up. Sadie's voice asks the caller to leave a message after the beep.

'Hi, Jay? This is Pamela Krowsky over at Executive Placem—' But I'm already across the sticky floor, reaching with both hands for the phone next to the fridge.

'Pam. Jay. Sorry, I was out in the yard. What can I do for you?'

'Jay? Oh, hi. I was calling to let you know that the Deltech guys really, really liked you.' My erection gets harder. 'I mean, they thought you were wonderful, just wonderful. Felt you showed real leadership qualities, impressive skills. Loved the slogan you came up with.' At long fucking last. 'They were very impressed with your experience, felt you really grasped their market space. Said you really, really knew your stuff.' Damn straight. 'Unfortunately.' My dick starts to go limp. 'They've decided to go with the other candidate.' I slide down against the fridge and sit down in a puddle of cheese. It's warm. 'It was close this time, so don't let it get you down. You know these things take time.' A year? Hang in there, Jay. 'Hang in there, Jay.' Something will turn up soon. 'Something will turn up soon.'

I leave the phone on the floor and return to the living area. I grab my gear and head over to the sofa. I drop the J&B and notepad onto the seat. Just pretend the phone never rang. With the tumbler squeezed against my torso, I rummage, one-handed, in search of the remote control. Booze spills down my Go Team Fuck-Up t-shirt, joining the other stains. Beneath a folded pile of clothes, under a pile of dirty laundry, I find the remote.

I settle into the middle of the leather sofa, in the maximum shit-shovelling vantage point. The cheese on my boxers is congealing. I pull the pad closer and going back to Number Four, I scribble: 'Subsection 4(p): Say *Cheese*'.

I pour another stiff drink, slug it down, and slam the glass onto the coffee table. I pull one of the folded shirts out from under me and raise it to my nose. My smell test confirms it is part of a minuscule pile of clean clothing lurking underneath the nastier contents of the couch. Must be remnants from the load I did last time I made a list. Right around the interview. I scoop up a few t-shirts and a handful of rolled socks and toss them onto the coffee table, making a mental note to take them upstairs sometime; whenever.

I snap on the television. Confronted with sports vs. politics vs. porno, I settle on the latter, taking care of the most pressing business first. See? I'm still capable of prioritizing. Afterwards, I pour another drink and jot down Number Six: 'Get expanded cable reinstalled'.

Com'on Jay, stop dicking around. I snicker. The J&B is kicking in strong. Don't waste your slots on such trifles. Especially ones that can be categorized under a more important main section, like, 'Get a life', for example.

Trifles? Peanuts, chicken feed. Don't start, man. Well, would you rather think about the fucking job you didn't get? Okay, okay, calm down. We can play for a little while. Jejune, nugatory. Why the other guy? How do you know it was a guy? Maybe it was some hot shit, lipstick, MBA chick. Jay…Don't. Don't what? Just do the words. Otiose, there. Com'on, something with a P? Paltry! What else do you have? P, r…u, v. V? Vapid. Vain. Good one, double entendre, extra points! W? Worthless.

The words make me want to play Scrabble. And Scrabble makes me want to be with Sadie, in a cabin in the woods near Tahoe, just the two of us, exhausted after a long day of skiing. Too tired to make love – we do that in the mornings before hitting the slopes – we lounge in front of the fire, sipping red wine, playing with words, playing with each other.

Sadie said we could work things out. 'But you have to stop. You have to come back to me.' She'd slammed the car's trunk shut. 'Back to the world.'

I snow-globe so hard I see actual stars. Focus, Jay, focus. Do the list, watch the screen, drink. Drink, don't think.

'Get a new body in just three weeks!' a ripped man on TV yells. I clasp my glass between my chin and chest and lift my t-shirt to look at my stomach, something I've been avoiding for months. I pinch the roll. Two-and-a-half or three inches? Where oh where has my six-pack gone? Where oh where can it be? I snort into the glass. Gone to pot has my potbelly gone. Need to change the ole spare tyre. I slap my stomach – hey there, buddy-boy – and snort into my glass again. I reach over for the pencil, planning to write: 'Buy Abflexor' and the 1-800 number, when my paunch manages to push a button on the remote. A Matlock rerun. My buddy-boy-belly has changed the channel all by himself. Clever boy. I dig out the remote lodged between two fat rolls. I've lost the will to complete the information. Instead, I write: 'Check website'.

This leads me directly to Number Eight: 'Knock off the chat rooms. HUGE waste of time'. I add three exclamation marks for good measure. '!!!' But. I love the chat rooms and they love me back. This will be harder to implement than remembering to brush my teeth. Online, I'm handsome, successful, I have a job; I even have a goddamn six-pack. I am the man I used to be. I'm the man Sadie loves. Loved? No job, no girl, no prospects. I shake my head until it pounds. Jesus, am I causing permanent brain damage?

Sadie.

Sadie, Sadie, Sadie.

Refusing to cooperate, eh, brain? We want to wallow do

we? Indulge The Jay? Bask in self-pity? Think about sexy Sadie? Dream about kiss and make up? Sadie and Jay sitting in a tree? Well, man, it's not going to happen. I snap the pencil in two and bombard the man in the too tiny shorts on the screen. Come up with something else. I glance frantically around the room. Anything. Just keep going, don't stop and think.

'Water the plants,' I roar, rising. I storm over to the corner, grab the once green palm and hurl it across the room. Earth and dead fronds fly through the air. The base connects with the mirror above the mantel. Shards of silver shower down. Seven years of bad luck? One down, six to go! Yippee Doo Dah, I scream and punch the air.

I grab some clothes off the sofa and toss them around. The cushions are next. They bounce against the ceiling before landing in the chaos spreading across the floor. Now I really *do* need to get the carpet cleaned, I whoop. I snatch the tumbler off the coffee table and throw it with all my might – Mighty Microwave Masturbating Man, Me, to the Power of Five M. Mach Five, baby. It tumbles through the air – so *that's* where the name comes from – and smashes into the glass door at the far end of the room. The glass cracks down the middle. The coffee table is next. Bottles, magazines, mail, mugs, socks, one flip-flop.

'Want another one?' I shout, retrieving the notepad from under a cushion. My hands tremble as I claw at the pages, shredding them, destroying the list. I dance a jig as I sprinkle the pages of yellow confetti, a loon rain dance. 'Nine! Get the

27

goddamn window fixed,' I bellow, pumping my fist at the ceiling. I jump wildly onto the sofa, tipping it over. I tumble over the back and land with a crash. I thump my elbow.

'Motherfucker!' I clutch my elbow and jump to my feet. 'Fuck you. I won't. I can't.'

Ten? *Ten?* I eyeball the room.

Deadweight, decay, debris, destruction. Drunk.

I'm a goddamn pathetic drunk.

I sink to my knees, still clutching my elbow. Tears form behind my eyes. Jesus, Jay, you're not going to cry, are you? I try to blink them back. Boohoo, Lil' Jay got a boo-boo? I start to whimper. Christ, what a mess. What a goddamn mess. I fold into myself and, with my forehead on the floor, I start to sob.

A long time later, I lift my head.

Mister James Jonathan Jordan, I think as I look around the room, this is your final chance. This is it. Do Number Ten for her, for me, for us. Get your goddamn shit together. Get a job, get back to the gym, get a fucking life.

Slowly, an ecstatic grin spreads across my face. I scrounge around until I uncover what's left of the notepad. I find the nub of the pencil behind the TV. I pull one of the black leather cushions closer, dusting off some earth, and prop it against the overturned sofa. I lean back against it and with the pad on my lap, I start a new list.

'A Ten-Point Plan To Win Sadie Back.'

Number One? I tap the pencil against my chin. After a while, I start to write.

'No. 1: Brush teeth every day.'

This time, I get up. Slowly, I climb upstairs. In the bathroom, I squeeze tri-coloured paste onto my toothbrush. I brush for two full minutes. Front, back, deep into the hard-to-reach places. I watch my mouth in the mirror while I work. I spit and drink water straight from the tap. I glance back at the mirror, at my unshaven chin, my mouth, my nose. I force my gaze upwards, and, as I meet my bloodshot eyes, I reach for the floss.

Next Door

Pippa Griffin

Day One

The man and the woman next door are having sex. Not wild, urgent, heady sex, but weary, grinding, heavy sex.

She listens to the woman grunting with every thrust.

He lies next to her, also listening, although neither of them has admitted as much to each other yet.

The woman next door is getting louder.

He coughs and shifts in the bed.

He's heard it, she thinks. – They're having sex aren't they, she says.

– Yes, he replies. – It sounds like it.

They lie still in their double bed, listening to the heaving woman next door. She hears the man groan as the woman sighs. The man must be more excited, she thinks.

He tries to remember the last time they had sex. She wonders if listening to other people having sex is making him want sex. She wishes the woman would hurry up and come, she would like to go to sleep. He thinks there was a time when listening to someone else having sex would have made both of them want it.

The man and the woman next door are grunting at the same time. She pushes her head further into her pillow. He wonders whether squeezing her hand a little would give her the wrong idea. He decides against it. There is a final heave from next door, the man and the woman are done.

She turns to him. – At least we can sleep now, she says.

– Yes goodnight, he says and they turn their opposite ways.

Day Two

It is six thirty in the morning and she is woken by the man and the woman next door having sex again. She listens harder this time, sure that he is asleep beside her. She can listen without feeling guilty. She can listen without thinking about what she is feeling.

The woman next door is making the same noises as last night. She listens to the woman's chest being squeezed as the man next door bangs inside her. She realises that the woman next door isn't thinking about being heard. The woman next door has no other thoughts or distractions. She wishes the thoughts in her head could be forgotten or ignored.

He is still asleep, snoring gently. She wonders who the man and the woman are next door and what they look like. She thinks they must be on their honeymoon – perhaps this is why they are having sex for the second time in twelve hours. She tries to count how many times she has had sex in the last twelve months. She rounds it up to three.

The groans of the woman next door are louder and more urgent. She thinks she might like to try sex again but she has forgotten how to start it. She moves her hand down between her legs and curls her pubic hair around her fingers. She doesn't remember hearing any foreplay from the woman next door, then she realises she's not sure she knows what foreplay sounds like anyway.

The man next door wheezes.

She thinks the man might have a heart attack. She wills the man on, holding her breath, listening to the woman's rhythms and feeling her own pulse against the pressure of her unmoving fingers. The man and the woman next door moan together, their bed banging against the dividing wall.

He stirs from his sleep.

She turns away, snatching her right hand from her thigh and using it as a pillow to her left cheek.

His arm flops over the ridge of her waist. – I love you, he murmurs. She doesn't move. She shuts her eyes, a tear rolling onto her pillow.

Day Three

It is three o'clock in the afternoon and he has gone to the bedroom to fetch another bottle of suntan lotion and the camera. He would like to take a picture of her sunbathing. He likes the way the sunlight skims the curve of her belly, it makes him want to reach out to her. He knows this isn't going to happen today, so he has decided to take a picture instead. He steps inside the bedroom, leaving the door to slam behind him. He rummages in the drawer for the camera.

He moves to the corner of the bed. He is tired yet he is not sure why. He lies back, staring at the ceiling. He is not sure if he is having a relaxing holiday or not. He has finished his second book. He has never read so fast. He is finding it easier to read than to talk. He thinks she might feel this way too. Every morning when he wakes up, she is already lying next to him reading. He can't decide if this is because her book is so good, or if talking to him is so bad.

The man and the woman next door have started having sex.

Their every whimper feeds the anger in his groin. Three times in three days. He wonders how many other times the man and the woman have had sex without anyone hearing. He frowns as he looks at the ceiling. He is angry that they are having sex for the third day in a row. He would like to have sex, any sex, any day of the week. The anger rises within him. – Go on then old man (he is convinced the man next door is old), fuck her, he says out loud. - Fuck her hard, fuck her for me.

The man and the woman next door do not speak, they just growl and grunt. He listens to the woman's panting and imagines it to be hers instead. He unbuttons his shorts, shuts his eyes and matches his rhythms with theirs. He sees her on top of him, her bikini bottoms pulled to one side where he is pushed inside her. He watches the weight and curve of her breasts move with the rise and fall of her hips. He watches her shut her eyes, tip her head back, mouth drop open. He feels her lean forward, her hair falling across his cheek, her nipples pushing against his chest.

He groans with the man and the woman next door and all three of them fold in on themselves.

He wonders if they have heard him. He wonders if she is

36

wondering where he is. He feels too warm to wonder too much.

Back by the pool, she wonders if she has brought enough books to see her through the holiday.

Day Four

They are sitting on their balcony reading. Every now and then, she lowers her book and looks at him over the cover hoping that he doesn't notice. He has read the same page five times, memorising the patterns of words. Every now and then, he moves his book to the right and looks at her beyond the corner of the page, hoping that she'll notice.

They pretend to read like this for about an hour before realising that the man and the woman next door are not having sex. They are not on their balcony either.

– Which couple do you think they are? she asks.

– Which who are? he replies, trying not to let her think he's thought about the man and the woman.

– The people next door. The people who are always having sex, she says.

– Yes, he says, unsure what to say next, unsure of what she will say next.

– I think it is that odd couple, the lady with the spiky blonde grey hair.

– I'd rather not think about it, he says. – If it is her, then it must be him, the fat guy with the rosy cheeks.

– That would explain how he got them! She laughs. She's laughing, she thinks.

– Yes, he says. She's laughing, he thinks.

They return to their holiday books. Hers is about shopping, a romance. His is about mass murder, a comedy.

– Is the book good? he asks.

– No, she says. – There are lots of people having sex.

He is looking at the balcony floor. He would like to look her in the eye, but her eyes are so dark and deep and sad and hurt and scared, he can't. Her eyes will make him cry.

She would like to look him in the eye, but his eyes are so full of light and hope and longing and pity and fear, she can't. His eyes will make her cry.

– I love you, he says, raising his head and daring to see.

– I know, she says, not meeting his dare. – Likewise, she says.

A door slams. The man and the woman are back.

– Shit, she laughs. He laughs too.

– Want to go back to the pool? he says.

– Probably best, she says.

Day Five

They have been eliminating guests from their enquiries all morning. He thinks it might be the old couple who don't wear rings on their wedding fingers because he saw them heading towards the corridor. But he is not sure if old people still have sex and he doesn't want to think about wrinklies having sex too much. She disagrees. She thinks it is the couple where the woman is much younger than the man. She thinks this explains why the woman next door is always the one who makes lots of noise, whilst the man's pleasure is stifled, silent. She thinks a younger woman would have less inhibitions, although she stops herself halfway through this discussion because she is thinking about her inhibitions and her silence.

— Do pubes go grey when you get older? she asks.

— I don't know, he says.

— I found a KY Jelly coupon cut out of my grandmother's *Woman's Own* once, she says. — How often do you think she had sex?

— I'd rather not think about it, he says, pulling a face that makes her laugh.

— But isn't it amazing that they still fancied each other at eighty, she says.

— I fancy you, he says.

She starts to smile, frowns, then dips her head towards the floor. She moves one foot on top of his and leaves it there a moment.

— You've got hairy toes, he says.

— No I haven't! she says giggling.

— Maybe they'll go grey when you're old, he says.

— Then we'll see if you still fancy me, she says.

— I will, he says, counting the seconds her browns hold his blues. One, two, three...

Day Six

Down by the poolside, they watch as an elderly couple help each other up from a hard morning's sunbathing. The man is overweight and has thick, raw stripes on his back where his flesh has pressed through the slats in the sunbed. The woman has varicose veins bulging through the backs of her knees. They decide it can't be them as the woman carries a walking stick, even though she is panting like the woman next door.

A young couple approach the terrace. The woman has dark hair and plump breasts. The man is fair, toned and slim and follows in the woman's shadow. The woman wears a leopard print bikini of triangles and ties that cut her hips like a string-bound beef joint. The man wears tight trunks that cup his balls and tell the world he dresses to the right.

They watch as the couple jump into the water, swim and kiss, swim and kiss. He watches the woman's breasts bob and press against the man's chest at the end of each length.

She watches the woman's smile after every kiss and wonders if the man is hard beneath the pool's surface.

He wonders what it must be like to have those breasts moving up and down above you. She wonders if the woman can feel the man's erection, and if she might see it when the man climbs out.

— I'm going to the room, do you want anything? he asks.

— Yes, she whispers. — Yes I do.

Day Seven

The woman and the man next door are having sex. Not wild, urgent, heady sex, but quiet, gentle, steady sex.

The man next door talks to the woman as they make love.

The woman next door gasps and says the man's name.

The man and the woman next door listen as the woman and the man next door come together, the wall separating their pleasure from their pain.

There is a Saviour

Wayne Price

Leyden had seen her naked once, slipping out of his son's room in the small dark hours of a winter's morning, padding catlike to the bathroom door. It was towards the end of the school term and he'd been working through the night, bleary-eyed and wired on caffeine at the kitchen table, marking exam scripts. She'd glanced up the long hall towards the light but hadn't noticed or hadn't cared about him staring back at her over his stacks of papers. Embarrassed, he'd got up and moved out of sight of the hallway, then waited a while after the flush had been pulled to be sure she'd had time to flit back.

That had been early in her stay, just a week or so after she'd moved in to share a room, and bed, with his nineteen-year-old student son, Matthew. After a long, bitter quarrel with the boy that had made him feel morally petty for objecting to the girl's arrival, he'd finally given in, realising, even as they raged at one another, that a part of him was intrigued by the idea – was hungry for any change in their deadlocked, fierce life together. After saving face with a few petty rules and restrictions he'd allowed the two youngsters to get on with their arrangement, secretly fascinated.

To his surprise, he'd soon found himself actually enjoying

the extra presence in the roomy, unhomely Edinburgh flat. Though he rarely saw the girl, Emma, other than in passing, and even then never exchanged more than a few polite words with her, he sensed a contentment about her, a stability that seemed to make the flat a busier but much more placid space than it had been before. The ugly silences he'd often endured with just Matthew for company became almost a thing of the past, though the boy still communicated only when necessary, and never with warmth. Above all, Leyden enjoyed having the tokens of a woman's presence around him after years of living without them: the bewildering toiletries in the bathroom, pastel buntings of underwear on the radiators, the scent of lotions or perfume sometimes lingering in the hallway.

Then, after six peaceful months, without warning Matthew decided that Emma had to leave. Typically, the boy had explained nothing but asked Leyden, in a tersely written note pinned to his bedroom door, to drive her home to Kettick, a small fishing town on the east coast. It would be a four hundred mile roundtrip at least, Leyden knew, maybe half of it on slow country roads; but his son had never learned how to drive and over the winter months the girl had moved in much more than she could manage on a train or bus. Gripped by a fury he couldn't fully explain to himself, Leyden had stalked through the flat, hoping to find the boy alone. But the couple were out or lying low behind their locked bedroom door and for the girl's sake he resigned himself to a long, embarrassing journey.

That Saturday morning, Leyden collected the hired van he'd booked and drove it back through a cold, light drizzle to the pile of luggage, boxes and plastic bags Matthew had brought down from the flat. The youngsters were standing watch over the boxes, careless of the rain. They stood hand in hand, Leyden noted, and a surge of distaste towards his son made him turn his face away as they approached the van. There was a bang against the side of the vehicle – the flat of a palm – and he heard Matthew shout for him to come and unlock the doors.

Neither of the youngsters seemed willing to make eye contact with Leyden as he joined them on the pavement and unlocked the van's big, sliding side-door. You should get in the cab out of the wet, he said to Emma. We can load up.

Ignoring him, she detached herself from Matthew and took hold of one of the suitcases. A freshening breeze was tugging at the plastic bags amongst the boxes, rustling them, flinging cold drops of heavier rain.

Okay, Leyden said, as if to himself, and began lifting and loading alongside her. For a few moments the boy watched them, blankly, then followed their lead.

Once the loading was done Leyden climbed inside and waited at the wheel while they got through their goodbyes. The rain, strengthening all the time, had begun to drum onto the roof of the cab and when she heaved herself up into the passenger seat Emma's long dark hair was lank and dripping. She gasped as she sat back, wiping the wetness from her forehead. There was a whiff of spirits on her breath and

Leyden looked across at her, searching her face for signs of what to expect in the hours to come. Her smooth, distracted face gave nothing away. As Leyden indicated to pull out from the kerb she squirmed to stare out at Matthew and Leyden, despite himself, glanced across at the boy also. His thick black hair was glistening. Hunched and grimacing under the downpour he offered up a perfunctory wave, and Leyden again felt an upswell of exasperation and shame.

Thanks for the lift, she said, turning from the window once they were out of sight of the tenement.

He shrugged and cleared his throat. Listen, he said, I'm sorry about all this – the way he's acted. He wet his lips. Getting you home safe and sound is the least I can do. The collars of his shirt and jacket were wet through after the loading and as he moved his head to address her he felt the cotton rub cold and coarse against his throat. She wasn't looking at him; she was looking straight ahead. He turned his own eyes back to the road and shivered. The rain was washing down hard onto the windscreen and the inside of the glass was clouded with moisture from their wet skin and clothes. It was hard to see out into the traffic. He turned the fan heater to high and the cab filled with the sound of rushing air.

Shifting in her seat she stared hard at him for a while. There's no need to be sorry, she said, raising her voice to be heard over the fan. Matty just needs some time; then we'll get married properly and be back together again for good.

Surprised by the authority in her voice, Leyden glanced across at her. You think so? She nodded once, decisively.

Well, that's good. If you think you're ready for all that.

She made no reply and in the awkward lull Leyden was suddenly aware not just of the heater's loud blast of air but also, behind it, the churning electric motor driving the windscreen wipers. He listened to it flailing the blades against each swill of rain. He knew without looking at her that he had made some mistake.

You don't believe me, do you? she said abruptly. You think I'm just being young and naïve.

No, he said. I didn't say that. He turned the fan down to a lower setting. He could feel his temperature beginning to rise and, with a finger, loosened the damp collar of his shirt where it stuck to his neck. She was still facing him, he realised, though he didn't turn to make eye-contact. He caught another trace of alcohol on the stuffy air and wondered grimly how much she had drunk.

Matty told me you don't believe in anything, she said casually, as if noting the weather. He said you're too bitter. He told me you're the most cynical person I'll ever meet.

For a long, stunned moment, Leyden replayed the girl's words in his head. He heard himself laugh, humourlessly. Heat was spreading over him now, prickling at his scalp and neck. Did he? he managed to say. He nodded as if in approval. And what does Matthew believe in then?

She was doing something with her hair. Out of the corner of his eye he caught glimpses of her bare white forearm rising and sweeping back. She took her time answering, then said simply, Matty's very spiritual.

49

Spiritual! he almost blurted, but checked himself. He nodded again instead, labouring for some response that might put a quick stop to the conversation.

That's why we've got to be apart for a while, she went on.

Leyden realised he was still nodding, and stopped himself. Matthew was always the…serious type, he managed at last.

At noon he turned off into a service station and asked her if she was hungry, taking a close look at her face again. She had pulled her hair back tight over her scalp, knotting and pinning it above the nape of her neck. She looked white and distant and shook her head when Leyden repeated the question.

Well I'm getting a coffee at least, maybe something to eat, he told her.

I'll go to the Ladies, she said, opening her door.

Okay – I'll be in the Burger King. He followed her through the rain across the car park and into the foyer.

He was already eating at one of the window tables by the time she came to find him. She eased herself into the cramped seating opposite him and smiled. She looked better, Leyden thought – there was colour in her cheeks.

I was sick, she announced. I had a drink this morning before we left. She laid a hand over her stomach. I feel fine now, though. I'll get a burger too.

I'll get it, he mumbled through a full mouth, but she was already freeing herself from the table.

Across from him a burly, shaven-headed man was struggling into his seat. His thickly muscled arms and neck were blue with crudely drawn tattoos – a death's head, slogans in gothic script, swastikas. The man ate slowly, thoughtfully, staring straight ahead.

Emma returned with two small plain burgers and a milkshake. She bolted them quickly but neatly, dispatching one after the other with just a few swift, precise bites. Once the food was gone she slowed down, dawdling over the drink. Twice Leyden caught her eyeing him as he turned from staring out at the rain. She smiled briefly each time and then looked down at her drink, or across at the skinhead's tattooed arms and neck.

Still feeling okay? Leyden asked finally.

Much better. I just needed to be sick. She laughed self-deprecatingly.

He smiled, glad that the silence was broken.

She stared at the skinhead again for a while, then turned back to Leyden. How long were you married? she asked casually.

Leyden frowned but managed to keep smiling. He reflected for a while, looking sidelong at her open, strangely impassive face, realising with some surprise that he felt a growing sense of pleasure at the thought of being open, perhaps a little vulnerable, with this peculiar, awkwardly mannered girl. Maybe somewhere inside her, underneath all the callowness, lay a seed of sympathy, even recognition. The thought pleased him, but in a way that made him shift nervously in his plastic seat. Fifteen years, he said.

That's a long time.

He shrugged, faintly gratified by her response. It sounds a long time when you're young.

Her mouth twisted into a half-smile and once again he knew he had slipped. Sensing what was coming next, he braced himself.

Why did it go wrong? She took a draw on her milkshake, her eyes fixing him. Do you mind me asking?

No, he laughed. No, I don't mind. It's, ah, water under the bridge. He paused as if to reflect though he knew exactly what he was about to say. He cleared his throat. We just married too young, etcetera etcetera, you know. The old story. To his surprise he realised he was blushing and his chest had grown tight.

She was nodding but her gaze was penetrating now, maybe puzzled, Leyden thought, or maybe critical. He shifted again in his tiny seat, wishing he'd never let the conversation happen.

But if you'd been right for one another, then marrying young wouldn't have mattered. She placed her milkshake on the table between them like a checkmate.

Leyden regarded her. Well. She was kind to me at a bad time in my life, he said. That can mean a lot to you when you're young. Too much, probably. He shrugged. Anyway, people make mistakes. And people *change*, he said, glad to have thought suddenly of that final, conclusive truth.

She screwed her face into a quick sceptical grimace, then relaxed it. After a long pause she said, I think it's good that Matty and me have broken up for a while now. We'll be stronger because of it when we get back together. With her fingertips she shifted the tall paper beaker of milk across the table in small zigzags. Matty thinks so too. He said he never wants to do to me what you did to his mother.

Leyden winced. So that's it, he thought. That's what it's all about. Back to the boy. Of course – it should have been obvious to him. Well, I don't know, he said dully. But we ought to get moving.

Outside, the rain had eased and as he walked between the rows of parked cars to the van Leyden felt grateful for the fine, needling coolness it brought to his face. Ahead of him he recognised the shaved head of the tattooed man. He was covered by his jacket now and was getting into a white van like theirs. A sudden cold slap of wind made Leyden shiver and he jogged the last yards, hearing her footsteps keep pace on the wet tarmac behind.

In the cab of the van he sat still for a few moments, gathering his thoughts while she rearranged her hair again, this time freeing it from its knot but then tying it back into a long, slack ponytail. She half-turned her head, eyeing him obliquely. I had alopecia when I was little. All my hair fell out.

He met her gaze. She was slicking her hands over her scalp now, over the tight wet strands. Oh, he said.

It used to come away in clumps. I'd be playing with my hair and stop to look and my hands would be full of all this long black hair. You never feel it coming out. She smiled oddly at him. I screamed the first time it happened.

He turned back to face the windscreen, feeling suddenly

53

too tired for words. But he had to speak, he supposed. What was the cure? he said at last.

She shrugged, still smoothing around her skull. It was just nerves – it went away in the end. She yawned. Did you see the man at the table next to us? With the tattoos?

Leyden nodded, finding himself yawning also, triggered by the girl. Shut up, he needed to tell her, but of course he couldn't. Shut up now, please, and for Christ's sake just let me drive. He sighed.

It's really weird. Matty told me a story just last week about someone exactly like that – a skinhead, really violent and racist and everything. His minister told him about it.

His minister?

At his church.

Leyden closed his eyes. Oh, Christ. What church? What minister? He listened to her voice tumbling eagerly on, light and life in her face for the first time that day, and wished he could get out into the cool rain; maybe lie under it; let it wash down and drown out all this embarrassing nonsense. Through a kind of daze he followed her story about a tattooed young skinhead cut out of a car wreck by a black fireman. The fireman saw his Nazi tattoos and witnessed to him about Jesus, she was saying, while he was cutting him out. He had to keep him talking to keep him alive, this black fireman. He was the only survivor – she'd forgotten to say that, at the start. And he was a minister now, in London, she was telling him, using his tattoos as a witness. He could have had them removed but he used them as a witness, now.

Leyden grunted. There was silence for a while. Finally he slotted the key into the ignition.

You don't believe in any of that, do you? she said.

He felt himself frown.

I'm not saved either. But at least I've got an open mind. How can you explain what happens to people like that otherwise? If there isn't a saviour?

Leyden opened his mouth but said nothing. Why was she provoking him like this? Every time she opened her mouth, another trial, another challenge. Some kind of displacement, maybe. Anger at Matthew. Yes. It had to be that.

But you don't know, do you? Just because *you* don't believe doesn't mean there isn't anything to believe. Maybe there is a saviour.

Maybe, then, he said at last, losing all patience. I don't know. But even if there *is*, he spat, his voice rising helplessly, what the hell would *he* know? What the hell would *Matthew* know about it? He twisted to stare her down.

She drew back into her corner but forced a hard, thin smile. That's a terrible thing to say, she said quietly. And don't shout at me.

He breathed a miserable, embarrassed laugh and a gust of wind swept the car park, quivering the van. He waited a minute or so, letting his head clear. Sorry, he said, and started the engine. Turning to her, he saw she was close to tears.

Matty said you were a bully. And a coward. Her voice was strangled but she swallowed hard and carried on. I always thought that was a mean thing to say. But now I think he was right.

Leyden frowned. I don't care what he thinks, he said firmly. I don't even know what he means. Listen, he said, he's thrown all kinds of shit at me over the years and it doesn't stick any more. He paused for a while, staring out at the car park. The skinhead in his white van was still there a few rows ahead of them. He hadn't even started his engine. What was he waiting for? Leyden turned to face her. And it doesn't matter to me what *you* think, he finished.

Her eyes narrowed a fraction and a flicker of gratification passed through Leyden like a current. Well it's obvious what *you* think, she blurted. It's obvious you think I'm stupid because I'm too young to know any better. But maybe you're the stupid one because you're too old.

Too old for what? Despite himself he began to laugh.

To listen to anybody else! It was her turn to play fierce now, he realised, and his laugh set into a grim smile.

I don't know. Whatever, he said. Then, studying her again, and curious suddenly, how old *are* you, anyway? he asked.

She took an old wadded tissue from her jeans pocket and blew her nose wetly. Sixteen, she said through cupped hands.

What?

Nearly seventeen.

Leyden blinked as if shaking off sleep, a sharp thrill of alarm twisting his stomach. Christ! he said.

So? she challenged, but without confidence.

I didn't know that. He breathed in and out once, slowly. If I'd known that I'd never have let you move in with him. Sixteen! Christ! he said again.

56

She snorted but shifted uncomfortably in her seat.

How can you be at university? I thought you met Matthew there?

I never said I was. I said I was a student. I'm doing my Highers at Telford.

Highers! He shook his head, a tight, angry grin locking the muscles of his face.

It doesn't matter.

It matters to me!

It's none of your business.

None of my business? He shook his head, a strange, excited outrage uncoiling inside him. You lived under my roof like a married woman, all these months, he said, hearing his voice rise in pitch again, and you're just a kid…just a wee *girl* for Christ's sake.

I'm not a child! And you can let me out if all you can do is shout at me again. She shrank away from him, bracing herself against the door, but made no attempt to open it.

He took a deep breath, trembling, shocked at his own arousal. Now that the first hot flare of prurience was dying away he had a sudden sensation of absolute clarity. Everything she'd said that day, every absurd statement, every gesture and inflection seemed to replay in an instant behind his eyes. Just a kid. Of course. All the bizarre mystical arrogance – just precociousness. Just childishness after all. A kind of helplessness really, he thought, and felt a sharp pang of superiority and pity towards the frail, cornered creature at his side. An acute consciousness of his male, adult bulk swelled within him, a sense of his heavy flesh and bone, full grown; all its stolid, controlling power. Well, he said, and looked her in the eye. Do your parents know? What do they think about it? He opened his mouth to question her again but stopped himself, not trusting his voice to conceal his triumphalism now.

There's only my father, she said flatly.

Oh, he said, and paused. So what does he think?

She leaned her head against the window and didn't answer.

I know what I'd think, he breathed, and shook his head.

By the time they rejoined the motorway she was sobbing freely and as he listened to each long, shuddering release it occurred to Leyden that in the wake of his new mastery over her, what he felt wasn't anger or disapproval, nor just simple pity for the way he'd made her feel now, but something more like foreboding; like dread. What were these passions she had stirred up in him? How had she known how to do it? And why do it, anyway? He understood women very poorly, he knew. How long had it been since he'd even spoken to a woman in anything other than a professional or indifferent way? Apart from a few half-hearted flirtations at work, and one awful, drunken humiliation – more years than he cared to number. Five or six, maybe. Nowadays, he rarely bothered making the effort to go out for anything other than his chess club and occasional concerts. Jesus, what was wrong with him? But was he lonely? Was he frustrated? No. Never. And what the hell was wrong with self-sufficiency, anyway? What was wrong with some quiet, adult dignity, in circumstances like his? What had caused this whole scene now, if it wasn't his own damned son's overheated, adolescent fever for every kind of intimacy?

An overwhelming impulse to remonstrate with the girl, to justify his chosen life – *chosen*, dammit! – was building like a blockage in his throat. He fought it back, unclenching his jaw, knowing the need was misplaced. She wouldn't have any idea what he was talking about. The very thought was grotesque; chaotic. But it was there: the urge.

And what had she meant by calling him a bully and a coward? What had Matthew meant by it? Years of learning to harden his heart against all that kind of blame and bitterness from the boy; why was it cutting into him now? Why a coward? A bully? He'd never hit the boy. Not once. Even through all the worst times when by Christ he would have been justified. More than justified! Who had he ever bullied in fact? One child, maybe. A cheeky, backward young boy he had lost all patience with in his probationary year of teaching. Just as the marriage was starting to fall apart, of course. No coincidence there, and he was green then, too, in his dealings with kids. Years of bank work had done nothing to prepare him for a classroom rustling with sniggers and whispers. He hadn't struck the brat, but kept him back and hurt him, yes, one day after class. Took hold of his collar hard and shook him off his feet like a pup, or a rat. Sheer luck it never came to light. But Matthew, no. Matthew he'd never hurt – Matthew who so often deserved it.

With an effort he woke himself from his trance. He was speeding and could remember nothing of the last few miles of road. Slowing the van he tried to relax his bunched, aching shoulders. It was sadness, not violence inside him, he thought, not danger. Dull, lumpen misery, and guilt for things he hadn't meant and things he couldn't change, like a great tumour on his heart. And who except Matthew would damn him for that? He opened his window and for a while let the sodden air rush in, chilling the cabin. Greedily he breathed it in, smelling the soaked earth, the open, indifferent land outside, letting his self-pity subside. Then he remembered her thin bare arms and closed the glass again.

Sorry, he said, but there was no answer.

An early, raw twilight was closing in on the narrow roads as they made the last stretch of the journey along the coast. After crying bitterly, but briefly, Emma had turned the radio on then slept for a long while, or at least pretended to. On waking she seemed calm again, even friendly, much to Leyden's surprise. She seemed content to chat to him, all provocation gone from her voice, pointing out the ways to ancient standing stones, the road to a fishing village abandoned since the war. Leyden made an effort to seem attentive, grateful for the changed atmosphere, but it was difficult to concentrate on her words or even his own thoughts. Now that she was speaking again the overwhelming gloom he'd felt earlier had returned, had found him out and taken hold of him like a tide around a tired swimmer, though he couldn't say why. Each time the great, grey shifting slabs of the North Sea hove into view he felt his heart lurch and chill as if his road ended out there amongst them.

Just inside Kettick he paused at traffic lights. At the crossing a small girl, oblivious to the rain, was swinging an empty plastic carrier bag out in front of her to catch and be pulled by the gusting wind. He could hear her shrieks each time she was yanked forwards. Other than the child the street ahead seemed empty.

You need to take the next left, Emma said. She was watching the girl too, but without expression. We're nearly there now, she added.

Soon they entered an ugly, unkempt cul-de-sac where the sandstone Victorian buildings of the High Street gave way to a cluster of modern, concrete-clad flats. There, she said, and pointed to one of the doorways. You can park right up close. My dad's too old to help with the unloading, she warned.

That's fine, Leyden muttered. He bumped the van up onto the pavement near the entrance then killed the engine.

She smoothed a hand over her hair. I'll go up and tell him we're here. Then I'll come and help.

Okay.

She hesitated a moment. He'll want you to stay for a while, to meet you.

Leyden stared at her, dismayed. I'd rather head back. Once everything's in.

He'll think you're rude if you don't. She opened her door and swung out before he could answer.

The radio was playing but had lost its signal somewhere along the coast. He hadn't noticed while they were talking, what with the noise of the engine and the rain. Now, alone and with the engine dead he listened to it crackling softly, unearthly in the gloom. He switched it off and lowered himself stiffly from the cabin. Wearily, he unlocked and dragged back with a long, low rumble the heavy side door of the van. He paused, leaning against the cold wet panel, then started hauling her stowed belongings out onto a narrow, sheltered porch. Finally Emma appeared, propping the door open with a box before stepping out to help.

He was sleeping, she said. He does want to meet you, though. You're to come up for some tea before you drive back.

Leyden puffed his cheeks. I don't know. It's getting late.

The tea's already made, she said. She crouched to lift a couple of boxes then started for the concrete stairs.

He grunted as he took the weight of a pair of suitcases, then followed her in.

The flat was on the second floor. The hall was badly lit and smelled strongly of tobacco smoke. The aroma was pleasant but somehow saddening and a sudden qualm of regret and loss swept through him. Almost overwhelmed, Leyden paused for a moment, as if to catch his breath, waiting for the strange, powerful feeling to pass. There was no sign of the father. She signalled to him to take the luggage into an empty bedroom to his left. He carried them in, wondering if the room had been hers before she'd left home. There were no pictures on the plain-papered walls or books on the shelves and the mattress on the narrow bed was covered by just a taut white cotton sheet. He slid the cases against a wall and was glad to get back out into the cold bright space of the concrete stairwell.

By the time they'd finished Leyden was clammy with sweat and impatient to be gone, though with a sense of guilty responsibility he allowed the girl to lead him along the hall into a narrow, low-ceilinged living room. Like the hall, the atmosphere was loaded with pungent, sweetish pipe smoke, obscurely familiar.

An old man began pushing himself out of his deep armchair as they entered the room. Here you are then, he said. Though heavily built, and obviously old enough to be the girl's grandfather, he moved easily to where the two of them stood. He held out a broad, doughy hand for Leyden to shake. Sit yourself down, he wheezed. He rattled out a quick, loose cough, his jowls quivering.

Leyden moved in the big man's wake to a low couch. Sinking into it he felt its broken softness draw him down and back. The father peered at him with a mild, sleepily satisfied expression, then followed Emma through a door into what seemed to be the kitchen. A big, boxy old TV in the corner was showing a football match, the volume turned down to a murmur. Directly in front of him an old-fashioned gas fire was burning fitfully, sputtering and hissing almost as loudly as the ghostly cheering and chanting from the game. The waves of heat from it were pleasant on his feet and legs. Yawning

63

hugely he sank back deeper into the spongy cushions and allowed his eyes to close. Jesus, he thought, I could blackout forever. With an effort he opened his eyes and forced himself to concentrate on the football. Soon the father was back again, handing Leyden a mug of strong, sweet tea. Well now, he said thickly, and lowered himself, grunting, onto the couch. There was no sign of the girl.

To begin with Leyden felt revived by the hot tea, but after the first few mouthfuls its heat and sweetness seemed to bloom inside him with the same narcotic force as the fire. He listened uncertainly, as if through a thick curtain of sleep, as the low, moist, unhurried voice of the girl's father asked him simple questions about the drive up, the weather, life in the city. Dully, Leyden answered him, hardly conscious of some of his replies. He was aware of the scrape of a match and the sharp brief stink of its sulphur, then the cloying fragrance of the old man's tobacco rolled across him like incense. Again he felt the pang of some hidden, childhood loss. Some long dead, forgotten figure, at the farthest edge of memory – not his father, surely, who had never smoked, or taken pleasure in any such thing, as far as Leyden could remember – but who, then?

See this, now, the old man said quietly, nodding towards the TV.

With an effort, Leyden lifted his slumped head and watched as the old man cycled through channels with a remote control. Satellite, ken? he confided. He stopped at a channel and gestured for Leyden to pay attention to it. It was pornography, but just a series of teasers for films showing later that night. The clips were so brief and close-up that Leyden found himself struggling to make sense of the glimpsed flesh and hard, concentrated faces.

Satellite, he heard the father intone again, soft and sly. Fae Europe, so it's double Dutch, ken? The old man chuckled, coughed wetly, then raced back through the channels to the football.

Letting his head drop back down, Leyden closed his eyes. He had to leave soon, he knew. If he let himself get any drowsier he'd have to find somewhere to spend the night. With each mouthful of tea, prickles of sweat were rising across his forehead. Hazily, he wondered if he was not just tired but sick; fevered, maybe.

So then, ye've kent ma quine a whiley now? The question was friendly but there was something measured, a hint of cunning in the tone that made Leyden straighten himself and concentrate on his answer.

Six months, he agreed. Since November. He cleared his throat a little nervously. Was this the beginning of the rebuke, father to father he wondered. He had already decided not to defend himself, or his son. He would listen passively, accept every judgement. Maybe he would stay completely silent through it all, rise calmly at the end and go. He didn't know. It was complicated somehow by her father being so much older than he'd expected. Battling against the warm fog in his mind he opened his mouth to speak, then halted, saying nothing.

Another match flared up to his right as the old man relit his pipe. And fit is it ye dae then?

I teach, he said.

Oho, a teacher, he said, and half-chuckled, half-coughed, rattling a thick chain of phlegm deep in his chest. So is that how ye met then, aye?

Leyden stared at the fire, his understanding slowed by its lapping heat and the billows of thick sweet tobacco smoke. He shook his head at last. No, no. It's not like that, he mumbled. We're not…

The father held up his broad, white hand and shook his head benevolently.

In Leyden's mind an image of his son formed, but it was featureless, like an effigy worn smooth. He had to speak about the boy, of course. But why did his own son's name catch in his throat now? And where was the girl for Christ's sake, to set the old man right? He felt his eyelids closing and forced them back open. Dimly, he was aware of the father saying something about tiredness, about staying the night. Leyden shook his head, but the old man was already up from the couch, moving away towards the kitchen.

What was happening to him? He was caught here, absurdly, like some drunken prodigal stumbling by accident on home. With a new sense of urgency he struggled from the clasp of the soft cushions to stand queasy and unsteady on the worn carpet. Behind a pair of heavy drape curtains near the TV he found a tall sash window and fumbled to open it, finally forcing it up a few inches. Outside the rain was falling straight, washing onto the van below, onto the street and onto the grey blocks of flats all around like the beginning of an endless, final flood. It was impossible to imagine the road home – when he tried, all he saw in his mind's eye was the rain, falling in swathes as if the journey lay not over roads and mapped land but a wilderness of water.

Sensing movement at his back Leyden turned to find the father at his elbow, staring impassively past him, out into the rain swept dark. The old man nodded. There now, mannie, see that, he said, his voice a low, complacent drone. There's nae call to journey in that.

The kitchen door opened and Emma stepped through, pausing there to watch the two men. She had changed into a plain white cotton shift that fell almost to her bare feet and her hair was bound up in a white towel. Like a kelpie, eh? Leyden heard the old man mumble admiringly. Like a kelpie fae the sea. She smiled distractedly and turned back into the kitchen again. As if obeying some hidden signal, the old man left Leyden and followed her out of sight. An image of the empty bedroom he'd carried her luggage into swept through Leyden like a chill. He saw the bare narrow bed again; the empty walls. He moved back to the couch and sat forward on it, hungry for the heat of the fire. Finally he sank back and allowed his eyes to close.

He woke suddenly, heart racing, from a dream of speaking with the ghost of his wife. He knew it had grown late. A solid darkness filled the gap in the drape curtains where earlier he'd stood. Aware of a presence behind him he arched his neck and saw the girl's face looking down at him. She smiled faintly as their eyes met and he slumped back into the cushions.

You were whimpering, she said, and he understood that she had woken him.

Leyden bowed his head. In the wake of his dream he felt a sense of renunciation and calm, though he had no clear understanding of what it was he might have renounced. The gas fire was still hissing at his feet. He tried to speak, but his dry tongue felt heavy and dead as sun-warmed wood or stone. Looking up again, he saw the silent bulk of the girl's father framed by the light in the kitchen doorway. Was he watching them? His expression was empty as a carved Buddha's. The eyes were open but it seemed the face of a sleeping man, face of all sleeping fathers. Leyden closed his own eyes, wearily, and knew he would not be leaving.

Of All Things

Anthony Cropper

My brother was seven years older and by the time I was born he had his own life.

Give me the child to seven, so the saying goes, and I'll give you the man.

The last time I saw him was in hospital. He was in a coma and his face was bandaged. A narrow window left his eyes visible but even they were closed. I sat by his bed, feeling like an intruder into his space.

We'd not seen each other in seven years, not spoken for almost as long, never sent cards or birthday wishes, we just got on with our lives, knowing that we both existed, but neither willing to make a move to talk or visit. He worked on the south coast for a communications company and had made his way into management. He'd been divorced for five years and had no children. As far as I knew, the lack of offspring was the reason for divorce. His ex-wife, Alison, had been desperate for children but none had arrived. Again, what little I know is that she now has a child, a girl, and she lives in France.

Our parents died when we were fairly young and I'm my brother's only surviving relative. I sit here, now, in his room, unsure of what to say. In truth, I feel I hardly know the man. We grew up together but were separated by our age difference. He was always distant, somewhere on the horizon, always through a window, going out, visiting friends, away camping or on school trips. And here we are now, forced together again.

Doctors rarely give any false hope, and this one told it as it was, giving all possible outcomes.

'He may survive, yes, but he could be brain-damaged, he might not walk, he might have a weakened heart…' The list went on and I wondered how it was possible for one man to have so many complications.

'So, it doesn't look good.'

'The internal injuries alone were severe.'

The doctor had a trimmed grey beard and wore thick-rimmed glasses which mirrored my reflection. He seemed way past retirement age but was still clinging to work. He'd had a lifetime of situations similar to this; giving bad news to the hopeful. What a terrible burden, I thought. All those tear-filled eyes. Mothers and fathers desperate for their children, desperate for this man to give them something to cling to. Words now spoken as matter of fact. These are the injuries, these are the possible outcomes. If A then B. If B then C. My brother seemed to have the alphabet.

'He may never recover from the coma.'

The journey to the south was six hours by car. I'd stopped at the services and called in the shop to buy snacks; drinks, crisps, chocolate. The shop had gifts and I wondered if there was anything I could take for my brother. It struck me then that I hardly knew him. I didn't know his taste in music or books, didn't know what clothes he wore, whether he liked football or cricket. I didn't know if he joked and laughed or was serious, contemplative. Did he drink? Did he smoke? Was he religious? How much had he changed over the years?

I looked around the shelves. All these terrible gifts, all these things and nothing suitable.

Simon had been on his own in a room for two days and by some miracle, someone, somewhere had found my number. Of all things, I'd been cleaning the windows, something which I'd never done before in my life. I heard the phone, climbed down from the ladder and was told the news.

I found Simon with wires to his chest, a drip in his arm, a tube up his nose. At the far side of the bed was a screen with four moving lines, differing colours, all frightening in their acknowledgement that Simon was still alive. For a while I just watched the screen, expecting a peak or trough, a continual loud bleep or cessation of all activity.

What do you do? What is there to do? Is it him awake and me asleep?

A nurse entered and noted down some information from the screen. She went to the window and straightened the curtains. She nodded at me and smiled.

'He'll be glad you're here.'

Of course, her saying that made me worse. I felt like a fraud, sitting here, feigning concern. Truth was, I was finding it difficult to know how I felt. I didn't know what to say or do, didn't know how to act, didn't know what to feel.

'Thank you.'

'Have you talked to him? It's okay. You can hold his hand, and talk. Some people are put off by all this, they think they need to stay away from the bed. Please. Push the chair up, don't be afraid. He'll be glad to hear your voice.'

'Is there anything I can do? Keep an eye on the machines? I could...'

She glanced at her fob, smiled, then left the room.

So there we were, together in our loneliness. I sat back in the chair and felt guilty that I hadn't done as the nurse asked. If he could hear, then maybe he was waiting for the sound of the chair being moved, maybe he was waiting for me to hold his hand. Could he hear? What would he want? Speak, brother. Tell me what I should do?

On arrival at the hospital I'd been given a briefing of his injuries.

'I'm afraid his clothes had to be cut away, all we found were these.'

The man handed me a small box which contained a wallet, a set of keys and a watch.

I sat with Simon for an hour, not saying a word beyond my initial hello and I was thankful when the doctor entered and asked me to leave. They needed time to take a closer look at his injuries.

'Get some sleep. Come tomorrow, whenever you like. I'm sure you've spoken enough for the night.'

Another feeling of guilt quickly rose within me.

'Would you mind signing this? Check his details and sign, please.'

I said goodbye and looked into the tiny window which exposed his eyes. They remained closed, lifeless.

'I'll see you tomorrow. Take care.'

As soon as I said that I felt ridiculous. What must the doctor think, me telling a man in a coma to take care? He's suffered horrific injuries, is fighting for his life, cannot even hear or see.

'Sorry,' I said to the doctor. 'Please. I don't know what I'm saying. You must think I'm a fool.'

The doctor jotted down some notes and glanced at me.

'Huh?'

'Saying that.'

'What?'

'Sorry. I'll go. I mean. I'm in the way. I'll go.'

Simon's flat was different than I'd anticipated. The place was a complete mess; pots and pans in the sink, unwashed plates on the table, takeaway cartons on the side. The TV had been left on, lights blazing, toilet used but not flushed.

This wasn't my brother. He'd always been tidy, close-shaven, showered, always scrubbing his fingernails, his bedroom had everything tidied away, toys in boxes, all stacked neatly. Everything had its place, shirts and trousers folded, but now, clothes spilled over drawers, the laundry basket a mountain, towels strewn about the floor. And there was a smell, not terrible, just something reminding me of slightly stale food or over-ripe fruit.

It was a small flat; one bedroom, sitting room, kitchen and bathroom, located on the sea front, at the top of an old hotel. The entrance was grand, but the building itself had fallen into disrepair. These may once have been decent dwellings and maybe some still were. But this, like I say, was different than I'd expected.

The window in the sitting room was the biggest surprise, it being totally false. When I first entered I thought he had a sea view, but no, the frame and view were just painted onto the wall. Curtains hung to the side, but this, this was bizarre. The only true window was in the kitchen, situated three or four feet to the left of the sink. It was a small square window, maybe three feet wide and it was open when I entered. I had to lean out, across the worktop, stretch as far as I could in order to pull it closed. And the view? It looked directly across to the sloping roof of the other side of the hotel, slates that were almost within touching distance. Leaning out, to the left, the side of the hotel and a small car park, to the right the gully between roof tops.

I picked up some of the rubbish from the floor, folded the towels and placed them over the radiator, pushed clothes back into drawers and closed them. I filled the sink and scrubbed at the pots and pans. I kept on at it for hours till the rooms were spotless, all the time pushing away thoughts of when we were young.

'Do I have to take him?' he'd say to our mother.

'He's your brother, you can at least act as though you like him.'

And off we'd set, him in a mood, stroppy with me for pestering to go.

'But he's just a kid.'

'And he's your brother. If he doesn't go, you don't go.'

When he left home I was nine going on ten. I never understood why he left so young. It was seen as being unusual, for him to take a flat just half a mile away and work in town. After he left he rarely came to visit. I never had the courage to ask if there'd been an argument, never picked up on anything, never heard raised voices or felt tension in the air, but, whatever, he left and the distance between us increased. After a couple of years he moved further away, first twenty miles and then not long later to the south coast where he stayed. Mother never went to visit, wasn't even invited to the wedding. He married in a registry office and sent a card, telling us of the news, saying as some form of justification that he'd not wanted for us to bother, that it would have been a big journey to make for such a small occasion. He sent a photo of the ceremony, just Simon and his wife with two other people and an old man, presumably Alison's father. Mother kept the photo on the sideboard for a week but then it was vanished away and even after she died I never came across it in her belongings. Simon had been in a coma for two days, but, in reality, as far as I was concerned, he'd been in a coma for years, we both had, the contact we had could not approach closer to zero.

Of course, now, I felt guilty for not trying harder. Would it really have been that difficult to ring and ask how he was? Would it have been hard to at least try for some connection, for some communication?

I used to tell myself that being brothers didn't mean any more than being friends or colleagues. We shared the same roots, but that didn't necessarily mean I had a stronger bond to him over anyone else. Why should I ring just for the sake of it? I should want, not feel burdened. All fine justification for laziness, for apathy, for forgetfulness, for fear. And yes, maybe there was some fear, fear of making the first move, fear of ringing, fear of saying hello to a relative stranger who happened to be my brother. In my mind, we had little or nothing in common. We had nothing to discuss. If I or he rang, it would be awkward and would leave us feeling insincere, hollow, inadequate. Maybe tomorrow, maybe next week, maybe next year.

We change and remain the same.

I finished tidying the flat and sat on the sofa. I wondered if he'd be pleased with what he saw or whether he'd say why, why did you tidy my space? Can you not see I prefer chaos? What gives you the right to come here and put order to my world? You think being my brother gives you some insight into what I want? Am I wrong to live like this?

In the morning I woke on the sofa. It was after nine and I couldn't believe I'd slept so long. I was still dressed in the same clothes, not even finding time to take off my shoes. I'd had a heavy, tar-like sleep and it was still lingering on my forehead, still pulling my eyes to close.

I was apprehensive about returning to the hospital. I checked the phone for messages but there'd been none. Before leaving I glanced over the flat; opened the fake curtains and switched off the lights. I was about to leave when I remembered the kitchen window. I'd opened it again when the stale air was getting to me.

I leaned over the worktop to pull the window closed but stopped to look again at the view. To the left, the small car park devoid of any vehicles. Out to the right, a slate-lined valley ending at an iron rail. Then, I noticed, along the roof, toward the end of the gully, a ladder. Lord knows why, but I pulled myself through the opening and stepped out onto the roof. The gully was about five feet wide, twenty feet high, maybe a hundred feet above the street. I climbed the ladder and once at the top saw the roof was edged by a small wall. Over the far side, a tall chimney and at the base of the chimney an old wooden stool. As I walked towards the chimney I was overwhelmed by what I saw. The view across the bay and out to sea was spectacular. There was nothing between me and seemingly endless space. Not another building could be seen. All before me was immensity; a limitless still, blue sea.

I sat there for some time, ten minutes, maybe longer and as I was about to leave, noticed a crevice between the bricks in the chimney. In the crevice was a small brown envelope and in the envelope a photograph.

I had no recollection of when and where the picture was taken but it was of the two of us, when we were young.

I'm with my brother and everything is black and white. We're both dressed in shorts, his hair's standing up on end and we're wearing big old football boots. My arm's linked with his and we're about to cross a road. My brother's chest is puffed out, as though he knows I'm remembering him, as though he knows I'm seeing him through all this impossible space. My face is dirty and he's holding a coat in one hand. The street behind us is empty, the buildings are tall and are filled with windows reflecting sunlight. There's nothing and no-one in the world beside the two of us. When I look close I see I've mud on my legs and I'm wearing football socks. One of the socks is pulled up, baggy round my knee, the other's hanging down over the top of my boot. My brother's grey jumper is tucked into his shorts and his smile is huge. I love him. Yes. I see and feel it clearly. Just look at us then and look at us now.

Then I remember a kicked ball and shattered glass. I'd wanted to run, to hide, to avoid confrontation, but he knocked on the door and apologised.

Listen, brother. There's things I'll never know and never understand.

For a moment I close my eyes and when I open them I'm standing on the edge of the building, looking over to the sea. The sky's bright blue and I've a feeling I want to take a leap into the void.

Once, we were young, and the world was not too bad. My

brother was and always will be with and of me and I know that in the end there's nothing but acceptance.

Today I'll go to the hospital. I'll sit by his side and will hold his hand and will tell him all I can remember about when we were young. I'll tell him why I always wanted to go with him and why I'd admired and looked up to him. I'll tell him all this and more. I'll tell him about my life, about what I like and dislike. I'll tell him about the view from his roof and I'll laugh as I tell him about my incomplete memories of our olden days. I'll tell him about how I'd wanted to phone, about how I'd hoped all along that *he'd* call. I'll tell him about our mother, about how she'd cried when she received the photo of his marriage, that she'd cried because she was happy. I'll tell him about anything that comes into my mind, about how I tidied his flat, about the takeaway cartons, about false windows and broken glass. I'll tell him about everything, and when I run out of things to say, I'll tell him some more, too.

Natural Causes
M Y Alam

Spending so long with folks more than double my age has its drawbacks. To new and narrow eyes they're all the same. Some feeble of mind, a few no longer in complete control of their bodies, but mostly viewed as old, past it and worthless. More to it than that. Always is.

The old timers I've known don't want pity, not from me, not from anyone, whether passing through or here for the long haul. What they do want, well that's anyone's guess. Nobody, as far as I know, goes to the trouble of asking them. They get on with it, biding their time, aware of the routines to live and die by. Nothing unusual, nothing different. Every day is Sunday. Every day is everyday, taking another ounce of flesh, another drop of soul.

Margaret had a sister called Linda. Linda died six months ago. Neither wanted to be here. Comes a time when even the hardiest soul can take no more of this place and the people who work it. The paperwork says natural causes but I got my own ideas. This is no murder mystery. In The Nightingale Care Home there are no serial killers. Being here, nothing else, finishes them off. And for nine years, the same thing's been killing me.

Nine years I been here, outlasting all comers and goers. A man gets less for armed robbery, I tell those asking how long

I been in this line of work. I got an interview the day I phoned up, enquiring after the advert in the paper. No application form filled, no references given, no certificates shown. A middle-aged turd with an Irish accent greeted me with a fake smile, a firm handshake and an over-friendly how-do-you-do. Teeth bleached white, belly corseted flat, face tanned two shades of Jaffa, I figured him for a one-time soap opera star, a TV presenter maybe. He pointed to the badge pinned to his lapel: Stewart Thompson, Home Manager. 'Call me Stew,' he smiled, radiating enough slimy self confidence to make me feel queasy, 'everyone calls me Stew.'

I didn't like Stew then. Nine years on I've learnt to loathe him. Digging his own hype in the biggest way, he considers himself gifted, wise and probably blessed from up on high. Each morning Stew wakes and walks up to the full length mirror in his bedroom. Smiling back at him, he sees a troubleshooter, a strategist, a visionary – the finder of solutions, the maker of decisions, the leader of men.

Showing little interest in what I said, he sprang to life when asking questions. *Why did I want a career in this line of work? What were my aspirations? What could I give the company?* Had I been brave and honest, I'd have told him I didn't realise this line of work constituted a career. My only aspiration was to stay alive, and as long as it paid me, I'd give the company my labour and nothing else. I needed a job. Any job as long as it kept me straight and off the streets. So I played along, spun him a few lines and made like an advert.

'Sounds good,' said Stew, marking something down on his pad.

'Thanks.'

'But you've no experience,' he said. 'No experience in this sector.'

I could have cracked him one on the chops for that. How the hell am I supposed to gain experience if no one gives me a shot? I'd heard this same line at every interview. The kind of shit that can drive a man crazy.

'But,' sighed Stew, then paused.

He studied me for some seconds, smiling but scanning my face for deeper information. Stew smiled like all men with plenty to hide. There's always something wrong with people whose smile is permanent. The ones who smile because they're happy, they're the worst. What is there to smile about? Life is not great, the world is not wonderful and people are not human. Not any more.

'I'd just like to say,' I said, sincerity coating every word, 'I won't let you down.'

Stew nodded to himself, pursed his lips and exhaled through his nostrils.

'That's what I want to hear,' he said, his smile broader. 'Congratulations.'

Stew didn't care a damn about experience. Turns out there's more personnel turnover in this industry than there is in cockle picking. They'll take anyone. As long as you have the right to work, can bear the measly wage, live with the unworkable hours and you're capable of holding a spoon and a conversation at the same time, the job's in the bag.

I've seen plenty come and go over the years. Some quit out of the blue while others stop turning up without explanation or warning. Some move on, find something better, maybe easier. People ask me why I stick around and why I don't find something better. I don't know what to tell them. I don't enjoy the work, not especially. The pay's lousy and I'm still where I started. Being here keeps me honest. You know what they say – whatever helps you sleep at night.

My old man got something terminal a few months before I came here. The collapsed lung, the emphysema and the COPD he could more or less cope with, but old age has a way of killing unlike any other. I expected him to quietly die, shamed into an early grave, while my life of crime added yet more sin to his scales. He hung on for as long as he could, wires and pipes invading him, sustaining his body but not so much his mind.

I turned up to the mosque for the Janazah, a scarf wrapped over the cuffs, one uniformed screw on my left shoulder, the other on my right. Cousins and neighbours offered their sympathies and I said nothing, for the first time in my life, realising the true meanings of honour, shame and remorse. So-called uncles shaking their heads, walking on by, thinking thank God their sons were turning out okay. Thank God they use me as a warning.

I only ever had one real uncle, my old man's youngest brother – over twenty years' worth of difference between them. A good man, what I remember of him. In his early thirties, smart and a bit of a real player and a ladies man, so rumour had it. Fit as a fiddle, my uncle, in his prime. Then one day he died. Natural causes. A heart attack brought on by nothing. We buried him local, my old man wanted that, so he could be close to him, visit his grave and all that. The night he got buried, I saw him in a dream. As ever, he seemed pleased to see me but he didn't say much. Didn't say a word, come to think of it. But he did give me something, pressed something into my trembling hands. When I looked, there was nothing. Thinking I'd seen a ghost, I woke up screaming, and pissing in my pants. My old man, having seen the same thing, just smiled and said: 'Never give them a thing, but always take what they offer.'

My old man, a fighter all his life, fought on even in death. Like his brother before him, he interrupted my restless sleep. Unlike his brother, he spoke, throwing the only spanner that ever stuck in my works: 'Take the better path,' he said. 'Don't promise me, son. Promise yourself.' Not many words but enough.

These days, ex-residents come and sit on the edge of my bed. Doesn't creep me out like it used to, but I can't say I like it. My hands instinctively clench, gripping onto and hiding something from them. I don't know what it is, this thing, but I know each of my unwelcome visitors want it. Six months ago Linda came begging and wanting and like all the others, she left, disappointed but understanding. Maybe I'm not scared like I used to be as a boy, but I always wake up sweating and shaking, praying it's the last time. It never is.

Every day I kick myself back into work but it's getting harder lately, each new shift a heavier burden to carry than the last. It helps when I remind myself of the hell it is for these poor bastards. Soggy cornflakes, cold porridge, rock hard toast, cheap vitamin supplements and cheaper orange juice gets their day rolling. An hour of burping, farting and worse follows. Next comes the first period of OS – *organised socialising*. OS isn't all that organised but no one seems too bothered. Get them all sat in a room and leave them to it. Some talk, others prefer to sleep but too many look around with expressions as blank as the day they were born, occasionally gurgling, now and then smiling at memories spent but not quite lost.

Tea and biscuits at eleven followed by activities. Knitting, basket weaving and painting by numbers. For the more adventurous, there's jigsaw puzzles with broken or missing pieces. On a shelf, on its own, sits a deck of cards that's been waiting years to be bust open.

Dinner's at one then another, much longer bout of OS. Like a chain gang, they're herded back into that stale smelling room, the television on with the volume turned down until five in the afternoon. The box is on again at six and off at nine, an extra hour on Friday and Saturday nights. On any given day, there is more tea, more biscuits and more boredom than any human being should have to endure.

Over the years I've picked up a few quick fixes and short cuts. I don't like myself for it, but it's hard not to succumb.

Why change the sheets when you can turn them inside out? Why mop the floors when a sweep is nearly as good? And when you hear them in distress, don't let it get to you because, according to Stew at least, tears are a form of therapy.

The very first trick of the trade I adopted, also one of the most powerful, is the ability to ask a question and to give the answer in the same breath. *Everything alright? Thought it was. Need anything? Thought not. Nice cuppa tea? Thought as much.* Never fails but there are days when I pray it would.

'Nice cuppa tea, Margaret? Thought as much…'

Margaret smiles her false teeth smile. I pour her a sweet and milky one.

'There you go.'

'Ooh, lovely,' she says. 'Just how I like it.'

Margaret is still a reasonably happy soul. Not quite worn down and out, but that'll happen, sooner or later. When she first came in, she'd laugh and sing all the time, knocking out big band numbers and Technicolor tunes only her generation knows, first crooned by stars now long since faded. But then Linda died. When someone dies, with them is a part of all those they touched.

Taylor, sat next to Margaret, has been here less than a month. They hit it off from the start and despite his own misery, he's been the reason Margaret has a smile back on her face these days. Not a happy man, Taylor. Lots of new arrivals have a hard time adjusting but this one's got it bad, much worse than most. This man sees the world in monovision, spends all day in a wheelchair and he's got a problem working his lungs. Won't let his condition fool me again, though. First day here, he jabbed me square on the nose because I told him we don't serve coffee. Two days later, he hooked one on Stew who'd been stupid enough to disturb his nap. Just last week he head butted the GP for no reason in particular. Today he's calm enough but I'm still on my guard. Sure, he's staring at the telly, but who knows what's going on between his ears.

'Nice cuppa tea, Mister Taylor?' I ask. 'Yes? Thought—'

'I don't understand this bollocks,' he says, his voice rough, raspy and, like a chainsaw, happiest when drinking diesel and dropping deadwood.

I look at the TV and see some small Scottish woman sticking her fingers into and then sniffing at a Petri dish full of human shit. Sick bitch should spend a week here if she likes that kind of party. Go wild, have herself a real blast. With any luck, she might even OD.

'Okay,' I smile. 'Cuppa tea? Sugar? Milk?'

'Don't like tea,' he states, still staring at the box, picking at the undersides of his molars. A single helping of sticky toffee pudding can last hours for those with too few teeth.

'Do we have to do this again, Mister T?'

He looks over my shoulder, then pans to the left, at some of the others doing nothing in particular. I had this man sussed the first time I saw him. A mean piece of work, a regular leader of the pack in his prime but those days are long gone. Misses his leather jacket, yearns for that oil-burning Norton but still hears a 1950s soundtrack following his every

92

move. Marlon Brando with a Yorkshire accent, a glass eye and a better grip on reality.

'Tea,' he muses. 'Nah. Don't drink tea. Haven't drunk that stuff since I were eight years old; not since nineteen thirty-three.'

He comes out with these lines every single time, and I am getting bored with it lately. In fact, today he's pissing me off. I wouldn't mind but I've another dozen still to serve, all fully conditioned and anticipating the next component of their day. Falling out of sync can throw even the most stable into a mild panic and no one wants that. If one of them gets all hyper, the rest are infected and in no time at all. The collective fear of chaos and disorder that follows can last for hours, days even.

'Must be some kind of record,' I say, following the script we've perfected over the last couple of weeks.

He looks at me, the colour in his real eye dulled with the onset of glaucoma. A former resident once told me only those who didn't, wouldn't or couldn't cry got cursed with cataracts. Getting on, but mentally as solid as ever, Taylor is a fighter, doesn't know when to quit. Been the same way all his life. Incapable of being broken, he quit crying before he quit tea. Trouble is, he's battling with the wrong man. I got no beef with him but he's a rebel. Wouldn't be a rebel if he didn't have a gripe with the whole world.

'Coffee,' he says. 'Only drink coffee. Black, no sugar.'

Coffee and people of Taylor's age don't mix. This is a scientific fact, so says Stew. Coffee is evil and if Stew had his way, the civilised world would be waging a never-ending war against it. Coffee does things, bad things, mostly. Keeps you awake at night but worse still, can make some people piss harder, longer and more often. Coffee, Stew believes, is a license to leak. One thing no one likes, especially visitors, potential residents and especially all those sons and daughters, is the smell of guilt, stale and thick, hanging in the air.

'So,' I start again. 'How about a nice cuppa tea?'

'You must be going deaf,' he says.

'You know we don't have coffee,' I explain. 'You know it's the rules.'

'Tea,' says Margaret, digging Taylor in his ribs. 'Go on. Nice cuppa never did no harm.'

Taylor gives her a smile, gently places his hand on hers and then looks back to me. With some reluctance he says:

'Go on. Make it good and strong, mind.'

Love blossoms even in winter. For some it takes years before they act, make their move, give breath and life to feelings for another. These two wasted no time and nothing keeps them apart. An unlikely pair but maybe that's the attraction: her petite, polite and still pretty; him big, bad-mouthed and brutal looking.

After tea, I check the mail. Taylor's notes arrived yesterday. Paperwork will get stalled on the desk of some pen-pusher who's too busy surfing for porn or buying and selling crap on ebay. I turn the pages until I hit the medical material. It's nothing short of a miracle that this old soldier is still living. Heavy smoker most his life. One lung now black, the other so damaged they cut it out. For the last sixty-some years he's been carrying a souvenir in his head; a piece of shrapnel from some foreign land. Not too many veterans of Taylor's type kicking around still. Honour bound, faithful to king, prepared to die for country. I wonder if they still make them like him. I doubt it.

He had an accident at home – slipped off a chair while changing a light bulb. A community nurse, an occupational therapist and his GP eventually referred him to us. On paper he's been heading for some kind of fall for a while. According to the experts Taylor is vulnerable. If he wasn't before, he will be soon, this place makes sure of that. A certain age – a *vulnerable* age – combined with an unfortunate event, no matter how minor, is all it takes. A little slip in the bath, one short fall out of bed, a quick trip on a loose paving stone and that's it, the family, the authorities, or both are quick to incarcerate, telling themselves and everyone else that *Dad can't cope any more.* Happens every time.

Taylor hates it here but he's not alone. Confusion and frustration reign in the minds of residents old and new. No one tells them why they're here and on whose say-so. A few still think this is a long session at a new day care centre. Eventually the questions about their pets, their bills, their homes and finally, their families will stop. That's when you know they've got the message. This is it, the last lap. Nothing except a body bag, a hole in the ground and a few nice words at the graveside to follow. When they know this much, they're as good as broken. And they always break.

Another death last night. The GP came first thing, took one look at the old girl and scribbled on the certificate as if signing for a transaction on his credit card: natural causes; that'll do nicely. Stew gave the order and within an hour, the room was empty of her and her belongings. What personal effects she had were bagged and waiting to be collected by the family or the local charity shop. Her body zipped to the undertakers, she'd be in the wind within the week.

In all, she'd been here nearly two years. Another one who'd been put to our kind of sleep. It's an uncomfortable truth but this is what we do. The relatives don't notice, don't care or don't dare speak. *After all, she* was *old*. It's never a shock when they hear the news. Could be I'm wrong, but I believe with all my heart that Stew gets a kick out of putting on his most sensitive voice and telling them how the Dear Old Whoever passed quietly during the night. I've seen him relish the words and heard him stretch them out, smiling to himself as he transmits and receives sorrow and pain through the telephone line. *Such a shame*. Sure. *So sad*. It always is, for someone. The loved ones mourn their loss but they don't question it. Dying is what old people are good at – decent innings, rest in peace, tasteful sympathy card and a mid-range wreath. They might buy the natural causes routine but they know there's more to it. Inside, they know. No use speaking up or down by that stage. Too late. Dead is dead and no amount of complaining and accusing will help. No point dragging this thing out any longer. Even if an autopsy does spell negligence, a medical blunder or something worse, nothing will come of it. Life will still have a hole, and living won't become any more bearable. Best not say anything and keep these thoughts inside. Best ignore the pain and bury the rage. Best let them rest in peace, at last and at least.

Stew calls me into his office the next morning. Rocking backward and forward in his executive model leather chair, he seems relaxed and content. He asks me to handle Taylor.

'I'm not sure about this, Stew,' I say. 'His health…he's been getting worse since he got here.'

'Afraid he'll hit you again?'

I could ask the prick the same question.

'He can barely raise an arm, let alone throw a fist. I don't think he can take it. She meant a lot to him.'

'All's fair in love and war, eh? I'd do it myself, but…I'm busy right now.'

I can imagine. Residents dropping like flies is not the best advert in the world. Spin and damage control is called for. He'll turn up to the funeral, say something long-winded and what he thinks is profound and towards the end, his voice will start to break. The son of a bitch might even shed a tear or two. Real slick.

'I'm delegating this very important task to you,' he says, as if bestowing some honour, 'don't let me down, now.'

I'm expecting something – a pointer or two, perhaps some good and effective words I could use. Typical of him to share nothing, not even experience. He looks at the door, then at me. He smiles. I can take a hint.

Not once in my nine years have I done this. Never had

cause to break such news. Always been Stew's responsibility, part of his self-defined job description. A few years ago he went on a course in sensitivity training. Seeing him in action before and after, I don't think he learnt anything from it.

I stand outside Taylor's room, turning words and phrases over in my mind, rehearsing the news, my apologies for breaking it and my sympathies. None of it's any good. How the hell are you supposed to say these things without causing pain? But maybe I'm missing the point.

I'll walk in and smile. Not a happy smile – not one of those stupid clown smiles but a polite smile, a doctor smile that tries to say *sorry, but it's bad news.* I close my eyes and hope that something comes. It does and it doesn't.

I see my old man, not Taylor, on the other side of the door, and force him to live through his final moments again. In bed, breathing shallow but loud, a mask over his nose and mouth, piping oxygen into him, a few pipes going into his arms, some wires stuck to his chest. Cold, might even be shivering. At his age, they always feel cold, no matter how warm they should be. Old bones, thin blood, tired soul.

I put my ear to the door and listen. After a few moments, a cough and the sound of a dying old man cursing himself. His body may be fragile, his skin bruises easily, but inside, beats a heart of stone. Old as dirt and harder than nails, he doesn't need kind and sensitive words or for me to go gentle on him. Old men like them took worse hits as boys, always seen them coming, straight from the hip. The amount of pain they fought, a little more at this stage in life doesn't matter.

They might not need to hear it gently but they need someone to be there.

Taylor squeezes his eyelids close together; helps him get a fix on whatever or whoever is in his line of single eye vision. His right hand rests on his left, the sound of the door closing makes me flinch but from him not even a twitch. I walk further in and glance around the room before turning to him. He looks in a bad way: miserable, tired and ready to die. Face blushed and marked with hundreds of tiny blue worms, the skin on his hands more fragile and more fine than rice paper. And above it all, like background music, the sound of a ghost in every breath.

'You,' he says, looking at the cup and saucer I'm carrying, raising a withered old finger at me. 'What's that…what you got there? You know I don't drink tea.'

'I know,' I say. 'It's not tea.'

It takes a few seconds of short, sharp and fast breathing before he gets the wind to continue, 'Oh. What you got for me?'

'Surprise,' I smile.

'Don't like surprises,' he manages, shaking his head, annoyed at his incapacity to even string one sentence together without taking a break for air, 'never have.'

I wait for him to catch his breath again. He's always like this. Even if he's only leaning back on a couple of pillows, his lung starts kicking him in the balls.

'Coffee. Black and strong. Thought you could do with a pick me up.'

'Pick me up,' he says, then coughs. 'Bit late for that.'

I don't know what to say.

Taylor nods and keeps on nodding. Nodding helps him regulate his breathing. His body controlled, his mind moves somewhere else, working a kind of thought that only comes a few times in a lifetime. He knows. Somehow, he knows. I don't know how but I can tell. Maybe, like me, he saw her again last night. Or maybe it's just a feeling gained, or a feeling lost. Something about her – her breath, her smell and her warmth – is not in the air this morning.

'Face like mine,' he says, panting. 'I didn't stay alone all these years out of choice.'

I put the coffee on the bedside table and stand there, waiting for him to speak, for something else to happen.

'She beat me to it,' he says, shaking his head, his breathing still regular, not laboured in the least.

In his face, in his body, I see the same look I see in the ghost of my father. Every time he comes, there is only hurt and no matter what I do or say, it can never go. That's the trouble with ghosts; they're not real and they're not even memories, just how they might have been.

Taylor's right hand clasps tighter onto his left, as if in prayer, now. His hands start to tremble, on his knuckles the skin pulls tight and thin, coated with a translucent sheen. In a blink but after a lifetime, he's changed.

And I still don't know what to say.

'She was a good woman,' he says, staring into the coffee, his voice strong and steady, telling himself more than he tells me. 'Fine woman. Damn fine woman.'

I suppress the urge to say something, to apologise and sympathise and do all the other things I thought I would. His rose petal eyelids close, and from where the eyelashes meet, a diamond is born and sparkles as it slowly rolls down his cheek. It pauses at the edge of his granite jaw, still holding and giving out so much light, but gradually it gains the will to fall onto his rising and falling hand. Comes a time when even the hardiest soul can take no more and wants to break free. I stay there, watching in silence until the moment his hand stops moving. When it does, the tear is gone, no longer a part of him and no longer a part of this place, and this kind of incarceration.

Persistence

Alexis Clements

Walking down the sidewalk I try to avoid stepping on the cicada carcasses that litter the path, their belly-up, twitching bodies cover most of the visible surfaces. The shoes are still nice and white – slip-ons, boat shoes, probably only a couple of weeks old, if that. In the past hour I've already managed to add a black streak to the top of the left one and there are creases now at the tips of both where the fabric has started to take on the shape of my toes beneath. But it's difficult to know if those creases weren't already there before, when I bought them, and it's only now that I've taken notice.

Two dollars I paid for the shoes, one dollar for each. I'm not entirely sure who would have bought only one shoe – all the same, that's how they were marked. I tried on a few other pairs from the quilted rack hanging on the inside of her closet doors before deciding on these. We wear exactly the same size, this woman and I, we even seemed to have the same funny tilt in our left heel.

I wasn't alone in the bedroom when I chose the shoes, there was a lady there with her child. The lady kept opening and closing the drawers of the bureau, feeling around in them with her left hand, searching for forgotten treasures, unmarked goods she could haggle over or slip into her bag unnoticed, loot from the dead woman's boudoir. Meanwhile the lady's little boy tried on a dusty brown hat that was hanging on a hook above the bed. It was an ugly thing, the hat, and too big for the child's head. It occurred to me, as he took it off, that it must have belonged to the woman's husband, who must have died a long time ago, but I didn't mention it. Instead, I went into the bathroom and looked at all the bottles of lotion and soap that sat in their scummy rings on the faux-marble counter. Ten dollars for the whole lot, if I wanted it. That was cheaper than the stuff at the sale last week, but I didn't use those sorts of things very often, so it didn't make any sense to buy them, someone else would come along for them – someone always did.

As I was finishing upstairs I heard a sharp buzzing sound in the bathroom. I thought maybe the woman had left some appliance running, something like a curling iron, used just a few days before, and now it was finally fizzling its way out. You never could tell how long ago the person died. There had been crumbs in the muffin pan that I was thinking of buying, I wanted to taste them, see if they were fresh, what kind of muffins they were, but the kitchen was crowded so I put the pan back.

She could have been puttering around in the kitchen just a couple of days ago. Bad hips maybe, or a heart attack. She was probably about my height, if I go by the shoes. If she was really old she would have had a hard time getting around the house, all those stairs and turns. It was probably that stubbornness that old people get, knowing that the lines are

106

forming to take them and all their things away. They carry on even longer, just out of spite.

The buzzing sound was a cicada that had managed to wiggle its way through the window in its death throes. By the time I made it to the bathroom he was dead. Must have been one of the males, it was still too early for the females to be dying. You could hear them all sexing away in the trees from inside every room of the house. The boys screwing themselves to death while the ladies went on for just long enough to gorge on leaves and lay their eggs, before joining the heaps of dead things covering the sidewalks and streets. One journalist said that there were millions of them that had been paved over since their last hatching seven years ago. That the streets and sidewalks that marked the graveyard of the lucky ones, meant a different sort of end for their friends below. I'm sure in a few more years time the ones that have made it will have figured out how to eat their way through the concrete and asphalt. Death is instructive in that way, I think. Cicadas and cockroaches will carry on forever, estate sales, concrete or none. Nature's even more stubborn than old people.

Crossing the street, I almost step into a muddy puddle left over from last night's rain. It's going to be near impossible to keep these things clean – I can't imagine how she managed it. She must have been one surly old broad. Although the shoes don't look so old. Maybe she bought them thinking she would survive long enough to wear them out a bit, maybe she expected that they would eventually get dirty, remind her of where she had been. A lot of the other shoes were older – still clean, well-kept, but older, more wear on the soles.

My mother hates the fact that I wear other people's things. It's the thought of their skin or dander, the physical reminders, the possibility of unknowingly swapping fluids with a stranger, that bothers her. I never spend much time thinking about it.

I buy them because they're cheap; because I like to see what other people have left behind; because I think maybe if they've lasted that long then I can too. The coat with the funny wrinkle at the shoulder that probably came from the owner's hunched back, the sweater with the elbows always slightly bent, the skirt with the nametag sewn in the waistband, 'Suzanne Hayward'. Maybe by doing this I'll manage to find some way to keep going, to persist, despite the fact that so many people are dying all the time. Maybe I'll live on like the cicadas and cockroaches, these white shoes and I.

Twelve Noon
Sophie Hannah

It was as if the sign knew more than I did. I stared in disbelief, wondering how I could have failed to notice it before. It was square, blue with white writing, attached to a slim grey pole that disappeared into the pavement in a raised hill of concrete.

If I'd spotted it I would have parked elsewhere. There was a single yellow line across the street. Ron's disabled badge was stuck to the windscreen of our car, but I was alone, unsure of the rules, and queasy with nerves after my first attempt at driving in nearly ten years.

I read the words again. 'Maximum stay 2 hours. No return within 2 hours.' I looked at my watch. Half past ten. I had set off from home at nine thirty, and the drive, which as a passenger I'd done many times, took about half an hour, so I must have parked at ten o'clock. Morrison's was less busy than usual, and I'd been so distracted that I'd managed to buy only two things: a jar of coffee and a packet of spaghetti. These I succeeded in obtaining only because they were the items Ron had reminded me about. I couldn't make any decisions: lager or wine, chips or potatoes. I tried to plan the week's meals in my mind, but my head reeled with thoughts of the other task I had set myself for this morning, the one I still hadn't done and might never do. Yet it was so important to me that I'd refused Ron's offer of a lift, in spite of my phobia. As recently as half past nine this morning, I had intended to honour the deal I had made.

I decided that instead of allowing the sign in its entirety to baffle and intimidate me, I would break it down into its two parts and consider each one separately. This calmed me somewhat. The first restriction – 'Maximum stay 2 hours' – presented no problem. It was the second limitation that bothered me – 'No return within 2 hours'. Taken together, the sentences were confusing. If I was not allowed to return to my car for two hours, that meant that I still had an hour and a half to use up. But if I also wasn't allowed to park for longer than two hours, then surely the sign as a whole meant to say that I must come back at precisely twelve noon.

I used to be an English teacher, and I imagined what I would say to the grey pole with the blue square head if it were one of my pupils: 'If "You may park here for exactly two hours, no more and no less" is what you mean, why not say so?' I hid behind this surreal fantasy for a few seconds. If the sign had been merely inefficient, I would not have been trembling on the pavement, unable to take a step in any direction.

'No return within 2 hours.' I tried not to leap to any sinister conclusions, but I could see no sense in this instruction. What if all one had to do was nip into Boots? Surely the sooner each space was available for another driver's use, the better. I shivered, feeling my skin prickle. The second prohibition made sense only in one context: if you were me, in my present predicament, with my particular dilemma.

The sign knew. It stood there, impassive on its one cylindrical leg, for me.

I hovered outside Gregg's bakery, with my Morrison's carrier bag in one hand and my handbag in the other. I forced myself to focus on my physical surroundings, to combat the unsettling sense I had that I was the only real component in an unreal scene, a breathing colour figure pasted on to a still, monochrome backdrop. Blood drummed in my ears. I tried to disregard it and listen outside myself, to the humming of car engines, the chinging of the till through the open door of the bakery, carefree conversations that hurtled towards me then left me, as suddenly, standing in their wakes. Fine rain settled on my face like mist. The sky was greying at the edges, darkening the morning. I tried not to take this as an omen of what might happen to me if I disobeyed.

For it seemed indisputable that the sign was ordering me to keep my promise. I had exactly an hour and a half, ample time. All I had to do was go to the Halifax, withdraw two thousand pounds and donate it to a charity. Simple. Why, then, were complications already tugging at the corners of my mind? I had never taken out so much money before. I had never had so much. The two thousand pounds was the result of six years of saving. Would notice be required for such a large amount? Would the people in the Halifax let me have cash or would it have to be a cheque? If the latter, I would need to decide upon a charity in advance, unless I asked them

113

to leave the top line blank, which I wasn't keen to do. The staff would be bound to eye me suspiciously: 'Two grand and she doesn't even know who it's for?'

My heart began to beat higher and faster as I realised that getting my hands on the money, in whatever form, was only the first challenge. What ought I to do with it then? Could I walk into one of the charity shops in town and hand it over without explanation? I doubted it; I was too polite to refuse to answer a reasonable question. I was also a hopeless liar. A fluttering sensation in my throat interfered with my breathing. I needed to sit down, even more so when it occurred to me that I ought not necessarily to restrict my choice of charity to those that had shops in town. In order to do justice to my promise, my decision had not to be based solely – or even at all – on my convenience.

It was all becoming too difficult. Waves of panic threatened to force all rational thought out of my mind. I dropped my handbag and my shopping on the pavement. This was the same feeling I had when I drove, the one I'd struggled with all the way into town. 'Are you sure you're up to it, love?' Ron had asked. 'I'm happy to take you in. It's no trouble.' Ron's kindness made my task so much harder. I would have to explain to him why the holiday that we had been planning for so long was now out of the question. That I knew he would forgive me made it worse, not better.

With a shaking hand, I reached for my car keys, thinking that if I could only sit down for a few moments, I might regain my composure. I was about to press the unlock button when it occurred to me that this could constitute returning to my car within two hours. Certainly sitting in it might. The immobile sign stared at me, each of its white letters an eye. Here, on the pavement, what if I was too close already? Would a traffic warden believe that I meant no harm, that I was only standing here in a sort of desperate paralysis?

It must be because these spaces were so few, so precious, I deduced. Evidently the council wanted to ensure they were only used by those whose business in town was substantial, taxing, and would take longer. The most deserving.

If I kept my promise to myself and gave the two thousand pounds to charity, that category would include me. I picked up my handbag and shopping and stumbled along the road, stopping when I reached a small, empty café called Mario's. I didn't want to be near people.

I ordered a pot of tea and sat at a red, formica-topped table with a scratched surface, counting in my head. When did I become so frightened of everything? It was difficult to pin down a particular moment; it had been gradual, like my aversion to driving. I would have found it easier to understand if, the day after Katie walked out, I had woken up terrified, doubtful of my ability to control either myself or the car. But it didn't happen that way. My problems began several months after I last saw Katie. One day when I was driving to work, I was careless and mounted the kerb. The following week I lost a friend's birthday present. It was around this time that I began to doubt my ability to cope. Ron started to have to make allowances for me, or 'take special care' of me, as he put it. 'I don't mind,' he said. 'You've looked after me all these years.'

He must have meant financially. His disability was not one that required physical care. Ron suffered from tinnitus. He had worked in a factory until his condition made it impossible. He hadn't had a job for fifteen years. I was the one who took care of our material needs. Not for long. Guilt made me wince. Yet a far worse guilt awaited me if I left the two thousand pounds in our holiday fund.

A young snub-nosed waitress brought over my tea. I pulled a notebook and pen out of my handbag, wrote 'Possible Charities' at the top of a blank page and underlined it. I must have looked intelligent and organised. At work, I had had a reputation for exceptional efficiency. Colleagues referred to me as 'a stickler'. Pupils did the assignments I set before those set by other teachers, knowing who would give them the sharpest telling-off if the work wasn't done. I reminded myself of this now, to bolster my confidence.

Choosing a charity was harder than I'd anticipated. The act of bestowing the money had to be utterly unselfish, with no benefit to me, not even a potential future benefit. This, I reasoned, would make my task even more agonising. Cancer Research was ruled out because I might one day be diagnosed with cancer, and, as Ron and I would soon be pensioners, Age Concern was a non-starter. I wrote 'NSPCC', then crossed it out when it occurred to me that Katie was bound to have children one day. And if she stayed with that awful man...

My heart, shrivelled from years of anguish, shrank still further. I would probably never see Katie's children. I could live with that, in the way that people learned to live with crumbling hip joints and debilitating migraines. What was intolerable was the thought that my unknown but nonetheless beloved grandchildren would grow up in the house of Toby Rollinson.

'Why don't you like him, Mum?' Katie had asked me, on what I now called the worst day of my life. It was the nineteenth of January, 1994. Every nineteenth of January since had been a torture to live through. I often wondered why anniversaries were so dreadful. It wasn't as if one avoided the pain for the rest of the year; it was there all the time. 'If you're worried about me not concentrating on my university work…'

'It isn't that,' I said.

'So it *is* something?' She knew she'd trapped me; I used language with more precision than most.

'Katie, I'm worried. You are…taking precautions?'

'Of course!'

'No, I mean…what contraception are you using? It's not pregnancy I'm worried about.'

She frowned. 'Oh. Well, you don't need to worry. We use condoms. And Toby hasn't got AIDS, if that's what you mean.' It was at this point that she had begun to sound indignant.

'I'm sure he hasn't,' I said quickly. Katie and I had always got on so well. I wanted to hear her usual happy voice again,

117

but now that I had started I knew I had to continue. Keeping it from her wasn't an option. Even Ron agreed, and he hated discord. He even worried about offending people he disliked, an attitude I had never been able to understand. 'But it isn't only AIDS you need to think about. There's herpes, chlamydia…'

'Mum!'

'I'm sorry. Katie, there's something I have to tell you. About Toby. You're not going to like it.'

'What? Tell me.' She wanted it over with quickly. So did I.

'He has sex with prostitutes. Young ones.' I could have said children.

Katie's face paled.

'I've known for five days. It's taken me this long to think it through. I needed to be absolutely sure that…'

'You're lying!' She had found her voice, a shrill wail. 'You've always hated him!'

'That's not true.' Though I'd had my reservations. The presents he bought Katie were never ordinary nice things. Without exception, they were brilliant ideas that made people comment on Toby's cleverness. A reproduction of the Mona Lisa, but with Katie's face. 'How did you do it, Toby?' everybody asked.

'One of the girls he…pays is a pupil of mine. She saw the photo of you in his wallet when he opened it. She'd seen you with me in town and knew you were my daughter.'

'She's lying! Maybe she knows Toby from somewhere else. Maybe she's obsessed with him and she's trying to wreck our relationship…'

I shook my head. 'I don't think so. It was very difficult for her to tell me. She made me promise I wouldn't tell anyone. Apart from you, and she said I had to keep her name a secret. She's one of my cleverest girls, Katie. She likes me.'

Lindsay Carter. Very bright and very poor. I sipped my tea, saying her name inside my head. I had kept my word and told no one. I'd lied to Katie slightly. Lindsay had told me it was her friend who slept with men for money, but I'd suspected it was her. If I'd tried to do anything about it, told the head or spoken to Lindsay's mother, she would have denied it. I'd had no proof. Perhaps I'd even been wrong; perhaps Lindsay really was talking about a friend.

After Katie stormed out, I was calm. I washed the dishes, expecting her to be back as soon as she'd confronted Toby and found out I was right. I should have anticipated no such thing. How complacent must I have been? That day was the last time I saw her.

She ignored all my pleas, even the letter in which I wrote that I had been mistaken and I was sorry, so sorry. I would have said anything. I went, several times, to the house she shared with three other students, but she refused to see me. Obsessively, as if I were in court in my own mind, I interrogated myself about how this could happen to a bond as strong as ours. When I thought back over the history of our relationship, I found no precedent, no tensions beneath the surface. We were about as close as a mother and daughter could be. Years later, I read about her engagement to Toby in the *Daily Telegraph*. His parents were just the sort who would waste money on that sort of nonsense.

Having crossed out 'NSPCC', I was at a loss. Amnesty International was a worthy organisation, but I couldn't be absolutely certain that I would never need its help. What if I were kidnapped by terrorists? One read about such things more and more these days. It was highly unlikely, I knew, but not impossible. Eventually I settled on the RSPCA. I had no pets and did not particularly like animals. To have to take my precious money and give it to an organisation that would spend it on dogs and rabbits would make me want to do someone an injury. It was ideal.

I paid for my tea and hurried to the Halifax before I lost what little nerve I'd mustered. When I reached the counter, I asked for a cheque for two thousand pounds to be made out to the RSPCA. I was astonished when the man behind the window said, 'RSPCA? Not time to book the holiday, then? Or is it already paid for?'

'Pardon?'

'I'm Terry, remember? Ron and I play bridge together.'

'Oh…of course.' My fingers gripped the desk. I would have to tell Ron straight away, otherwise this man might. I would have to tell him straight away because my nerves would not permit me to keep it from him.

'Ron showed me the brochure. I've never stayed in a five-star hotel.' His voice was full of admiration.

'Neither have we.'

'Ron says it's got three swimming pools.'

'Yes. I'm actually in, er…' I looked at my watch. I couldn't bear to hear the details of the treat we would have to forego.

Furious with myself for the ridiculous bargain I'd made and now had to honour, I allowed a voice in my head to say, 'It's not worth it.' Then I feared I would be struck down. What sort of mother would have such a thought, even fleetingly? I didn't mean it, of course, but Terry's musings on the Grand Hotel des Iles Borromes forced me to remember all those weeks in cold caravans, on sagging mattresses.

I was probably rude to him in my desperation to escape. Once I had the cheque, I went straight to the phone box outside the library and rang directory enquiries. Another call and I had the RSPCA's address. Before I had time to change my mind, I marched to the post office like a robot, where I bought an envelope and a stamp and did what was necessary.

Once the two thousand pounds was in the post box and out of reach forever, I felt the full horror of what I had done, what I could so easily have avoided doing. Only I would ever have known. I had told nobody about the deal, not one single other living soul, and the chances were my breach of it would have made no difference whatsoever. I believed in the notion of tempting fate enough to sacrifice our holiday, but not enough to be able to take even a grain of comfort from the idea that, having sacrificed it, I would be rewarded.

I staggered outside, weeping. People stared at me, but I found it hard to believe they saw anything but a shadow. Now everyone else existed in the realm of colour and sound and I was grey, silent, unreal; misery had made me invisible. I walked back to the Halifax and pressed my face against the window, wetting the glass. Beside me, a woman who was using the cash-point shifted to the right to put some distance between herself and the distraught lunatic. She completed her transaction and hurried away.

So eager was she to flee that she forgot to take her money. Time seemed to slow, as if the world needed winding up. I stared at the wavy edges of the notes poking out of the slot. Again, I had the sense that I was being shown something that was there for me alone. How could I be so superstitious when I was known for my rationality? I was a stickler. Everybody who knew me knew that I didn't watch horror films because I couldn't believe in ghosts or monsters, not even for two hours.

I reached out and grabbed the cash, noticing from the thickness of the bundle that it was quite a lot, certainly more than ten or twenty pounds. The woman was still visible. I watched her rush down the high street. She stopped when she got to Dandylion, a designer clothes shop for children. The incorrect spelling irritated me. I could have followed her and given her the money. Instead, I walked in the opposite direction, towards my car.

The sign was still there. It still said 'No return within 2 hours'. I looked at my watch. It was eleven ten. Fifty minutes to go. I stopped before I got too close and counted the notes in my hand. A hundred and fifty pounds. Disappointment wrapped itself around me. This would make no difference to anything. And I had done a terrible thing. I had deliberately stolen money and it wasn't as if I were starving. I had robbed a young woman I knew nothing about for the sake of a luxurious holiday in the

Italian lakes. Did this make me as bad a person as Toby Rollinson? I nearly vomited on the pavement.

But there was still time. The difference between a good person and a bad one, I used to tell my pupils, is that a good person tries to make amends. I crossed the road and ran towards the police station. I needed to get there quickly, in case the woman from the cash-point saw me. I didn't want to be caught by her before I'd done the right thing. How would I be able to prove my good intentions?

I had never been inside a police station before. The reception area was bland, beige. The woman behind the desk was not wearing a uniform. If it hadn't been for the police logo on the posters pinned up behind her, I would not have been able to guess where I was.

'I've stolen this,' I said, dropping the money on the counter, not wanting to touch it. 'From a woman, at the Halifax cash-point down the road. I can describe her in detail. You'll be able to get it back to her, won't you?'

'What do you mean, you stole it?'

'She walked away without taking it. She was in a hurry. I picked it up…'

'When was this?'

'Just now. Five minutes ago.'

'But…you said you *stole* the money. When, actually, you brought it straight here.'

'No. I stole it. I was going to keep it. I could have run after her, I…It was only later I changed my mind and decided to hand it in. I'm a thief.'

The woman sighed. I might have been crying. 'Not much later. Five minutes. Look, you've handed it in now, so there's no harm done.'

'There is! Theft is still theft, whatever the thief does afterwards. I should be charged just the same as any mugger would be.'

'Do you want to be charged?' She gave me a quizzical look.

'I…yes.'

'Why?' She leaned her elbows on the desk, slumped a little: plenty of time to listen to the confessions of a whimpering middle-aged oddball.

'I don't want to tempt fate by getting away with anything.' I was definitely crying by now. 'My daughter…' I wanted my daughter to forgive me.

'The woman was your daughter?'

'No, no…I…' I was too distressed to speak, and missed what happened next. The scene broke down into particles. I couldn't process anything properly. I had a vague impression of another woman appearing behind the desk, of being led into a room by the first woman, of being alone for a while. A warm Styrofoam cup was placed in my hands.

Following instructions, I sipped strong, orange tea. That helped. I took deep breaths, also to order. 'I'm listening,' the policewoman said. 'You need to get it off your chest, whatever it is.'

'I need to be charged with robbery.' My words were slow and tentative, as if I'd never spoken before. If I were to be sent to prison, however briefly, this woman would have to tell Ron what I had done and why. She could show him my statement. I wouldn't have to watch his face become a collage of crushed hopes when I explained that I'd thrown away our savings. And then Ron would have to tell Katie.

He hadn't tried to speak to her since the rift, not once. It was understood, assumed, that I would be the spokesperson for both of us. I was the one who dealt with words. My parents hadn't thought Ron was my intellectual equal. He was the one who did the driving. He should have forced me to get behind the wheel when I least wanted to. If he had, perhaps I wouldn't have been here now.

I would make him tell Katie, if he didn't think of it himself. 'Your mum's in prison. Because of you. Because she loves you so much.' It might make all the difference.

'Why did you steal the money?' asked the policewoman.

'My husband and I are supposed to be going on holiday in the summer. We'd saved two thousand pounds. It took years. We...we haven't had a night out or bought new clothes for longer than I can remember. The holiday was more important.' I cleared my throat. 'Anyway, today I withdrew all the money and gave it to the RSPCA.' A piercing laugh escaped from me. My account sounded so absurd. I half-expected to realise, suddenly, that I hadn't done it, that it was a hallucination.

The policewoman didn't smile. 'Why?'

'My daughter. She hasn't spoken to me for ten years. I tried everything, but...in the end there was nothing I could do apart from…what I did. Have you ever made a deal with fate?'

'How do you mean?'

'If this happens, I'll do that – that's the form they usually take.'

'Oh. You mean like, if I get this job I really want, I'll give up smoking?' She blushed. 'That was the only time I did it. I didn't get the job and I still smoke.'

'Yes. Well, I vowed to myself that if Katie – that's my daughter – that if she ever got in touch, I'd…give some money to charity. At first it was only a hundred pounds. The amount went up as the months passed, then the years. I thought that the more it was, the greater the chance she'd contact me. You know, because I couldn't bear to part with such a large amount…' Discussing it for the first time made me curious; what exactly was the rationale behind pacts such as mine? I had never examined this before; it had all been intuitive, almost organic. I hadn't asked myself *why* I would give money to charity if Katie got in touch. It seemed obvious. It went without saying. 'I suppose we make these bargains because we so fear that we won't get what we want, we feel a need to set up a consolation for ourselves. At least I can keep my money. At least I can still smoke. Or maybe it's an attempt to bribe the gods.'

'So your daughter got in touch, then? If you say you've already given the money away.'

'Yes…Yes.'

'Well, then.' She smiled, but I saw doubt in her eyes. I

knew she didn't dare ask me why, then, I wasn't elated, full of joy and relief. Why was I stealing paltry sums from innocent passers-by instead of celebrating?

I couldn't tell her. To say that Katie had got in touch was a better way to finish the story. It was the right ending: Katie wrote to me, finally, we were fully reconciled, and I handed over the two thousand pounds as promised. I was ashamed to admit to this well-meaning stranger that fate had made a fool of me. After all these years, the communication I received from my daughter was an article from the local newspaper, about her husband. His company had raised a large amount of money for a children's hospice. The story was accompanied by a photograph of a smug, bloated Toby passing a cheque to an elderly woman, his arm round her shoulders.

Katie hadn't sent a note with the clipping. If she had, it would have said, 'See how wrong you were about him?'

I knew perfectly well, and fate knew, that this was not what I had meant when I prayed for Katie to contact me. But I was a person who valued precision; I couldn't pretend that I didn't recall the terms of the deal, word for word: 'If Katie gets in touch, I will give two thousand pounds to charity'. I inserted no sub-clause about hostile, defiant communications.

The injustice was hard to stomach: that I should lose all my money in exchange for this. I tried to believe that Toby himself might have sent the cutting, not Katie, but I couldn't know for sure. And I couldn't risk trying to cheat. Fate would not catch me looking for a loophole.

I told the policewoman none of this. I feared I might disintegrate completely if I made it too vivid by saying it aloud, so I drank my tea in silence and listened as she told me that I would not be charged, that I should write to the RSPCA and ask for my money back, that I should be happy.

As far as I could see, I had only one thing to be happy about: I was doing the best I could to meet the demands made of me, as I understood them. I had given away our savings; we now had only three pounds and sixty-seven pence left in our holiday fund. I had handed in the money I stole and tried to secure a punishment for myself. I had not returned to my car within two hours. A reward for all this good behaviour might still be forthcoming.

I said thank you and goodbye to the policewoman and walked out of the building, trying and failing to feel free. I looked at my watch, saw that my time would shortly expire, and began to run. Then, because I'd sprinted too fast, I slowed down as I passed the bookmaker's and the bakery. I read the sign again. 'Maximum stay 2 hours. No return within 2 hours.' I had done it, complied with both requirements. I hoped this had been observed by the relevant authorities. As I pressed the button on the key fob to unlock the car, it was exactly twelve noon.

The Accessory

Paula Rawsthorne

There was no dapper man amongst the mourners, even after twenty years she would have known him. An overwhelming sadness washed over her; how bitterly disappointed Hilary would be.

It was back at the house, after the funeral, that alarm bells started to ring about Ophelia. Their Victorian semi was packed to the rafters with Hilary's transitory friends. However, in every room, they were distracted from their nibbles and wine as their eyes were drawn to all the spaces on the walls where Hilary's mirrors usually hung. Then later, when people made their pilgrimage up to her dressing room, they discovered that even the mirrored wardrobe doors had been removed and were agitated to see the hollow insides. 'Ophelia,' they inquired anxiously, 'where are all your mother's Gucci outfits and Jimmy Choos?'

'I've taken them all to the charity shop,' came the flat reply. Gasps of horror filled the room.

Colleagues at Jacob Sinclair Spa and Fitness were also growing increasingly concerned about Ophelia. It must have been a terrible shock to find her mother like that and they all agreed that after the sudden death of a loved one, grief can manifest itself in strange ways. They too felt bereft; in Hilary they had lost their most popular aerobics instructor but time was a great healer and that is why Jamie, Ophelia's manager, left it a full eight weeks before having that chat.

During his monologue he utilised all his interpersonal skills. He began by empathising with her obvious struggle to verbalise her pain and anger at her loss. Then he suggested that there were less distressing ways to show it, that wouldn't adversely affect their membership figures. He respected her too much to beat around the bush: she had let herself go! She was, after all, on the front line, the face of Jacob Sinclair and that face shouldn't be without make-up or, at the very least, her St. Tropez tan. Potential members wouldn't sign up with someone who had their roots showing and were positively offended by the small forests now sprouting from her legs and under her arms. Jamie pleaded with her to think of Hilary; the epitome of poise and beauty in her autumnal years. Hadn't Ophelia always been such a credit to her mother? He just knew that she wouldn't want to let Hilary down now.

Three weeks later Ophelia received a letter to inform her that, most regrettably, her contract had been terminated due to her persistent non-compliance with the company's standards and ethos. An unstoppable smile spread across her naked face.

Ophelia had been Hilary's pride and joy, the centre of her world, her greatest achievement. She told anyone who would listen about how she'd 'Single-handedly transformed what was an unappealing looking child into a radiant swan.' In their house of looking-glasses Ophelia could never escape her ever-changing image. Hilary would regularly inspect the reflection of her 'work in progress' whilst reminding Ophelia that, as mirrors were a girl's most honest friend, it was best to have lots of them.

As Ophelia grew up, she realised that she didn't have a personality: Hilary had, accidentally, suffocated it at birth with her own. So, Ophelia slid into her role as an accessory in her mother's drama. Her instincts quickly taught her to remain watchful and quiet and to keep herself in check, lest she upset her mother's fragile happiness. 'Does Hilary look beautiful today?' 'Does Ophelia love Hilary?' She soon picked up that answering 'Yes' would supply her with enough kisses and praise to sustain her through the times that she feared her mother might die of sadness.

Weeks of preparation went into Ophelia's annual portrait at Harvey's Photographic Studios. Twenty-one times an outfit had been painstakingly chosen, hair and make-up fussed over and poses practiced. Then, only after Hilary had agonised over the perfect shot, would she post it to her soul mate. Delivering it by hand had been out of the question for many years, as the threat of another restraining order always hung over her.

Hilary's bedroom was a gallery dedicated to the dapper man who smiled enigmatically from a score of photo frames. He could have been a 40s film star with his clipped, slicked-back hair and chiselled features. Ophelia would sometimes spy on Hilary dancing around her room, photo in one hand and a glass in the other, giggling at some imagined, flirtatious remark before bumping into the dressing table and swearing like a trooper.

For years Hilary had told her daughter that Daddy died when she was a baby – killed saving a child from the path of a speeding car. Ophelia knew this to be untrue but never questioned it as Hilary always seemed in raptures when she related the story of his heroic demise, adding more detail at each new telling. But to this day, Ophelia could feel the safety of the dapper man's huge hand wrapped around hers as they walked to the park. She could conjure up the delicious cocktail of pipe tobacco and Brylcream but also remembered the stench of Hilary's panic and desperation as the doorbell rang. She could still feel her cheeks being pinched and her pigtails being tightened until her scalp hurt. 'Oh so pale!' Hilary would lament. 'Now, big smile! No – perhaps best not to show your teeth.'

On these rare visits, her mother, make-up inches thick, hair and shoulder pads filling the hallway, would gallop in her towering stilettos to open the door, cleavage first. She'd insist he came in for a drink but the dapper man always kept his eyes firmly on Ophelia as he told the mother that he'd have her back by three.

On Ophelia's fourth birthday he came bearing a chunky doll that could wet itself. How she adored its wrestler's arms, bloated cheeks and piggy eyes, infinitely better than the Barbies that Hilary had provided to spy on her and to tell 'if you eat any naughty things that make you fat.' Ophelia kept these demonic dolls locked in her toy box.

By the time of her fifth birthday there had been no more visits from the handsome man and Ophelia had spent the day in her best dress waiting, as Hilary insisted that 'He'll be here any minute!' Her mother paced relentlessly around the house, refilling her wine glass and reapplying her lipstick, and it wasn't until ten o'clock that she allowed the bewildered child to get into her pyjamas and go to bed.

In the morning Ophelia couldn't find her favourite doll. She went to ask Hilary but her mother lay sprawled, fully clothed across her bed, snoring uproariously. Ophelia went downstairs to get her breakfast only to discover that the sitting room had been ransacked and behind the upturned settee she found the head of her chubby-cheeked doll, impaled on a fondue fork, with the letters B.A.S.T.A.R.D. scrawled across its broad forehead.

There had never been any mention of kindly grandparents or jolly aunts and it was when Ophelia was seven, and her mother didn't arrive to pick her up from school, that she realised that Hilary was all that stood between her and things much worse. Eventually two ladies came and took Ophelia to spend the night with a family where the parents seemed nice but the kids were not. One of them boasted to her that at his last placement he'd set the family's cat on fire. Another suggested that they played strip poker. Ophelia lay awake all night in terror. Hilary reappeared the following afternoon with no explanation but there were whispers in the playground that her mum had been locked in a police cell for threatening to kidnap Ophelia's dad's new baby. Ophelia's head spun from trying to work this out, but she felt excited that her mum was trying to get them a baby.

No baby ever arrived at their house but a presence entered it like a dark, oppressive storm cloud that prevented Hilary getting out of bed. This presence was a reoccurring visitor and Ophelia became adept at registering its arrival and battening down the hatches. During its stay there was no question of her going to school. She needed to make the glazed-eyed Hilary eat. She'd brush her mother's hair, clean her teeth, open the curtains and dance for her but the only thing that roused Hilary was the search for all the bottles that Ophelia would hide around the house. These bottles only made her mother sob and blurt out her festering thoughts. 'Of course, you know he'd still be here if I'd got rid of you. He couldn't keep his hands off me but once you arrived what was I left with? A screaming gargoyle, stretch marks and leaking tits!'

Ophelia's absences from school could be lengthy but were too infrequent for anyone to bother pursuing. And once Hilary bounced back, as she always inevitably did, teachers seemed satisfied with her vague explanations about a sickness that had plagued the house. Anyway, they only had to look at how beautifully turned out the child was, to know that Ophelia was well cared for.

Everyone agreed that there was no one more fun or gorgeous than Hilary when she was on form. During these times their house of mirrors would sparkle once more and Hilary would acquire new friends who'd take advantage of her hospitality, financed by generous maintenance payments and an array of credit cards. Often Ophelia would return from school to find her mother holding court, surrounded by salivating men and although she'd try to sneak past, Hilary would spot her and shower her with boozy kisses whilst announcing to everybody that this was her little princess whom she loved more than life itself. Ophelia would squirm out of her clutches and grab a handful of vol-au-vents before taking refuge in her princess's tower. When Hilary entertained into the night Ophelia would struggle to sleep but the times Hilary fell into despair, her child struggled to stay awake, terrified of what she might wake up to find.

At secondary school Ophelia attracted a flock of envious girls and at first she thought that they really liked her. They loved her style, they coveted her daringly high shoes and marvelled at her mask of flawless make-up. However, once they discovered that this was all her mother's doing, Ophelia simply became the gatekeeper to the object of their real attention. After all, she had a mother who insisted her daughter call her 'Hilary', a mother who took her on marathon shopping trips, a mother who had transformed her from a mousey-haired forgettable child into a blonde vision, so that even she couldn't remember what she really looked like. It was Ophelia who was the first in her year to wear contact lenses, to have manicures and waxing appointments. If only their frumpy, fun-hating mothers loved them enough to put them on diets and advise them that smoking was preferable to snacking.

It became worth inviting her around for tea in order to secure future access to Hilary. But when Ophelia went to their houses she was always unnerved by the order and calm, by the sensible mothers who greeted them, who checked for homework, asked them about their day and gave them hot meals and set bed times. These visits only confirmed her long held fear: Hilary was not like other mothers.

Her classmates spent their tea dates watching in awe as Hilary quaffed an exotic-looking cocktail whilst giving a masterclass in mascara. She really was so impossibly glamorous that the schoolgirls didn't even care that they left without actually having been fed.

It was when Valentines started to appear in Ophelia's schoolbag that Hilary had something tangible by which to measure her success. However, her pride was overwhelmed by panic and so, at fifteen, Ophelia was marched to the doctors to be put on the pill despite her protests that she didn't even speak to boys. 'Be prepared,' her mother explained like a conscientious Girl Guide.

When Hilary made it to parents' evenings the teachers tended to pause for a moment as they desperately tried to remember who Ophelia was. Then, with much relief, they would announce, 'Oh yes, your daughter is the one who always looks immaculate. Such a quiet girl, you'd hardly know that she's there; wish we had more like her.' Year after year Hilary was informed that, academically, given the encouragement from home, her daughter had the potential to do well. Hilary always reassured them that they could leave it up to her.

Ophelia found herself showered with presents when she failed to get enough GCSEs to go on to sixth form. Hilary found it difficult to disguise her delight that now there was no chance of her daughter abandoning her for some far-flung university. She consoled her dejected child. 'Haven't I always told you? It's beauty, not brains that gets you noticed in life.'

Hilary enrolled her at the local F.E. college which provided Ophelia with a Diploma in Leisure and Beauty and a chance to meet new people. However, any potential friends were soon hijacked by her mother who insisted on tagging along on their nights out. The evenings inevitably ended with Ophelia's peers gushing about 'What a riot' her mum was, as Hilary made a move on some alarmed looking young man. But for all her outrageous flirting, Hilary never took a lover: she always lived in anticipation of the return of her soul mate. And when he did come home, having left his impostor family, he would see for himself the wonders she had performed with his once plain, dumpy child and he would never want to leave his gorgeous family again.

Hilary was ecstatic when Ophelia got the job at Jacob Sinclair. She felt totally justified in having filled in the application form without telling her daughter. She knew her child and sometimes Ophelia just needed a little push in the right direction. And hadn't she been right about having those collagen lip injections before the interview? They had definitely sealed the deal. Now Ophelia could be surrounded by their kind of people everyday. Hilary longed to be a member but her credit just wouldn't stretch to it, so even though Ophelia didn't find her work environment exactly liberating, at least it was all hers. However, it was only six months later that she saw her mother gleefully tottering out of Jamie's office and Ophelia knew that her every waking hour had been infiltrated once more.

She was twenty-four when she met Joe. He was handing out leaflets in the town centre. He was a revelation! At first she was unnerved by his attentions, always encouraging her to 'Open up' and 'Let it out'. Her previous beaus had loved the fact that she rarely opened her mouth. They couldn't believe their luck when she would never stay the whole night because she had to get back for her mother. Joe told Ophelia that she was beautiful inside and out, that she'd lived under an oppressive regime and that he could set her free. Joe gave her strength, courage and she had faith that he was more than a match for her mother. So, a few weeks later, as Hilary plied him with gin and biscuits, he began his impassioned speech declaring that he and Ophelia were in love, they were going to get a place together, and although it was a generous offer, they wouldn't move in with her, even though he agreed her house was roomy and he knew that she wouldn't encroach on their privacy. Anyway, it wasn't like she wouldn't see Ophelia; after all, they did work together.

It took just three months for Hilary to get her daughter back, by which time Joe had discovered that he wasn't half the man he thought he was. 'It's for the best,' he mumbled as he helped Ophelia pack. Over those three months Hilary had spent more nights on their living room sofa bed than in her own house and when they did persuade her to go home it resulted in hysterical midnight phone calls about phantom intruders. At work too, Ophelia found herself constantly cornered by colleagues, frantic with worry about poor Hilary. They'd never seen her like this and even though Hilary had forbidden them from saying anything, they felt that she had a right to know that her mother just wasn't coping without her. Everyone knew how she'd devoted her life to Ophelia but she'd even been saying that she only wanted her princess to be happy even if it meant that she was plagued by silly thoughts of putting herself out of her misery.

'I'm so sorry it didn't work out with Joe,' sighed Hilary pulling the cork on a celebratory bottle of wine. 'Still, we'll always have each other.'

Ophelia noticed it just in time. Its gleaming surface caught her eye and she lunged for the banister, managing to hop over it onto the next step. She stood for a moment feeling quite shaken. Hilary must have left it there, she was always discarding things around the house. Ophelia had meant to pick it up but instead found herself walking out of the front door, shouting up to her dozing mother, 'See you at work!' And there, on the twelfth step of their Eiger-faced staircase, the mother-of-pearl hand mirror remained.

Jamie sent her home early from work. He said that she looked like she was coming down with something and her mind most definitely wasn't on the job. Maybe she and her mother had picked up some bug. She really ought to go and check on Hilary. She wasn't answering her phone. She'd missed two classes. The members were most put out.

The twisted body that greeted her at the foot of the stairs didn't look like her mother. The grotesque angle of her neck, the leg bent under her back, the splayed stiff arms; and her face! Hilary certainly wouldn't want anyone to see her like that! So Ophelia got her make-up bag and delicately blended blusher into Hilary's translucent cheeks before applying a wave of pillar box red to her blue lips and then, closing her mother's shocked eyes, she finished off with a warm brown over the veined lids.

It must have been a spectacular fall. The shards of mirror glistened on the stair carpet like fairy dust. Her heel had caused the initial rupture; embedding itself into the heart of the mirror sending shock waves out to the smooth mother-of-pearl casing, whipping her foot from under her and sending her flying down the stairs like a ski jumper.

Ophelia felt that there was no point in complicating matters. So she wrapped the shattered hand mirror in newspaper and put it in a neighbour's wheelie bin and then proceeded to vacuum up every last needle of glass. Once they saw the size of her stilettos, what other explanation was necessary? And how many times had her mother complained that her impossible heels were killing her, although she always added stoically that 'Beauty is rarely attained without sacrifice'.

Krupps XIXth
Michael Nath

One day, Joe, you would speak with him. You came down that way often enough didn't you, and in the afternoon he'd sit outside W8 at the table nearest the door. Those tables have a broad strip of green cloth beneath them, to look like grass. Full pukka in camel-coloured suit, yellow waistcoat, well-polished brown brogues, a silver pin in his tie of fine silk, there he would be. His eyes were the colour of the sea off Tenerife, his moustache as pure as a summer cloud.

You'd already taken to nodding at him when you passed; then you said, 'Afternoon!' and he said 'Afternoon!' back and raised his glass. The day came – you'd had a few beers somewhere or other – when you saluted him in the military fashion when you went by. It couldn't be long now. It may be the next time.

It wasn't the next time, nor the time after that, since the next time you were going one way in a hurry, while the time after that you were coming back worried. In fact, it wasn't until a day in August. The sun was hot and they'd put parasols above the tables. You got yourself a beer and said hello, so he made a gesture that you should join him beneath the shade of his parasol. His name was Johnny Mitchell. You introduced yourself as Joe Ward.

He was staying with his daughter just across there. On the other side of the road was a row of white houses. Johnny Mitchell's daughter owned number thirty-nine. There was a box with flowers the red of arterial blood on the first-floor windowsill. He'd come to stay with his daughter when his dear wife passed away in the new year. He was ready to go now; but his daughter would press him to stay a little longer.

The road was quiet, tree-lined, well off. He agreed to stay, just a little longer. The barmaid came out and asked if she could bring Mr Mitchell another drink. He said yes, just one more, a Campari, and a beer for his friend then drew a little square silvery tin from his waistcoat pocket and asked you if you took snuff. You had a short line off the back of your hand and it burned the passages behind the left face like chilli powder and mint dust. It was quite a sharpener, that snuff. Johnny Mitchell had a spot too. The little silvery tin was engraved with the words, Krupps XIXth.

'Had that made for me.' You watched his face, the eyes still young. 'RAF Conningsby. Sixty year ago. — Can you listen to an old man, Joe?' You nodded, eyes on his blue eyes. — 'Had it made as a souvenir. — Can you listen to an old bomber?' You could listen to an old bomber.

'Check this scene out, Joe. — August afternoon sixty year ago, low cloud lying over the base and the boys and I going along the path from the barracks to the briefing room, doing our best not to step on the cracks. There's a little lawn on one side, gravel bed on the other alongside the canteen wall. We are all of us ten times as het up as normal in our crew, Joe, on account of the fact that this is our last op.' Johnny Mitchell pointed his finger. 'All in all we've done twenty-nine, Joe, and after thirty you are free to live. After thirty, you are taken off active duty you see?' His voice was old, bright, as if sealed in varnish. 'We've lived through twenty-nine, and we can scarcely believe it. So many chaps we've seen lost. Imagine, Joe. The men you knew well this morning, you will never see again. – This is how it was. So many good men disappeared into the air.' Johnny Mitchell sat and remembered.

'Yes, we are pretty het up. If something can go wrong, it will. We don't dare to hope we will get to the end of it alive. And when we hear our target, we feel our number is up. – You see those briefings in films, Joe, but I tell you, they never let you know about the smell of men's insides. Every crewman is farting with fear.' Johnny Mitchell sniffed, concentrating brightly on you. 'We've been hoping for something soft: run down the French coast to La Rochelle, something of that sort. But they're sending us to Happy Valley. – That was what we called the Ruhr. It was a bit of black humour, Joe, when we said that, because the Ruhr Valley was the most heavily defended target area in Germany.' Johnny Mitchell paused. 'Some thought Berlin was worse, but I should say the Ruhr was number one, and nowhere was worse than the ground defences on the approach to Krupps AG. – This is our target.

'For the nineteenth time. – Eighteen times already, we've been over to blow Krupps AG to smithereens, and as soon as we get home, Alfred Krupp has the fucker on-stream again. We feel sure he'll have us before we have him. Nineteen's to be our unlucky number. – You know about Krupps, Joe?' You had heard of it, heard the name.

'My pilot was Frank Mason. Nose like this. Tall man. Flight engineer was called Dineage – forget his first name. Navigator was Dennis Wright, great pal of mine. He's dead now, Dennis.' Johnny Mitchell fingered his moustache. 'Wireless op – his name was Greatorex. Upper gunner was a Kiwi, rear gunner was a Welshman, Jack Morgan. – Who've I missed?' He'd missed himself. 'Ah – I'm the bomb aimer. – Farting like spaniels we are, Joe. Do you know fear like that? Do you know how the fear is?' Did he want an answer? There was a waft of hot cheese in the air from the kitchen of W8, blowing round the corner to where you both sat.

'You are in a seventeen-ton aircraft with eight Browning .303s that can knock a tree over, or turn a cow to beefsteaks in eight and one quarter seconds, and you are carrying ten tons of high-explosive ordnance, Joe; but when you fly over Happy Valley you feel as if you are walking down Piccadilly stark naked in the rush hour. Stark bollock naked.

'The searchlights play with you, Joe. Whenever they fancy, they can find you. Big cone of light playing on you. Fills the aircraft, the light. You are utterly exposed. You long to get back into darkness. If you are more than three minutes in the light, the ground defences will have a radar line on you. The flak is infernal.' – Let him tell of the flak, Joe.

'It is so thick, the flak, you can *smell* it.' How did flak smell? Did it smell of cheese? Bad breath? Melting metal? Sulphur?

'Won't forget the smell, Joe. – The splinters start coming through. Like knives. But a flak splinter weighs a lot more than a knife. Moves a sight faster than anyone could throw a knife as well. Flash ahead! Flash to port! Aircraft rocks. Then there's the stink and the knives come through. *Shtud! Shtud! Shtud!* Jack Morgan gets one in the face: 'Can't see anymore, boys' – I will not forget him saying that over the wireless. Voice as calm...as calm – he is in the tail, on his own, blinded. Then Greatorex takes one in the tooraloom, Joe. More or less castrates him. It is hell in there. You can smell blood, smell flak. You can see blood in the searchlight. Black splashes all over the shop. Smells of hot ink. Engineer gives Greatorex morphine to stop his noise, balls hanging down to his knee. No man can listen to that noise and do his job. It is hell, Joe. – Then we go through the gate.

'We've heard about this from one or two other crews. Isn't something chaps talk out loud about, for one reason or another. But it's said to happen when you're very close to the end.' Johnny Mitchell interlocked his fingers. 'It is like a feeling of freedom, a cold, free feeling. – I can find no other way of putting it.

'The skipper takes us down to three-thousand for the crack. This is asking for it, but we have no care. Our faces are burning cold from the outside air. Perspex has holes this size from the flak. I am singing something to myself, word for word. Know what it is, Joe? "I've Lost My Little Yo-Yo".' Johnny Mitchell began to sing quietly, blue eyes intent:

'I had it when I left the house at half past ten
I had it in my hand all right,
I showed it to the lady at the corner store
It filled her with delight…

'Like that, Joe. My mind is clear and I have no care. There are five or six big fires already from the first stream. Get my own bombs off very cool and calm. See them flash, Joe. On a marshalling yard, row of toolrooms. See them blow the pipelines to hell. I swear to you. From three-thousand feet I can see it all happen.' Johnny Mitchell sung again:

'The wife'll want to play with it when I get home
But I can't find it oh-no,
She'll take the only course
And sue for a divorce
When she finds I've gone and lost my little yo-yo…

'The song is going round and round in me, Joe. I am living for the moment, have no care. — We gain height. The fires are a long way under us, like red flowers and yellow, and at last we're out of flak range. Then we hear the guns in the tail. Over the wireless. On and on. He fires over two-thousand rounds, Jackie Morgan. He's blinded but there's a fighter on our tail and Jackie shoots the bastard out of the sky. Shoots his arse off. Saves our lives.

'We get back to Conningsby, Joe, and we start celebrating. But it is a queer sort of celebration.'

You went back the following afternoon. You'd been to drop something off at your sister-in-law's, so had to come down that way. How much did you want to listen to him again, Joe? You didn't know. Anymore than you knew if he wanted your company again. But he was there on his own. It was hot. There was a wind from the south. You weren't too keen to go home anyway.

'Had this made the day after, Joe.' He handed you the snuff box, Krupps XIXth. 'There was so much metal round the plane – shrapnel, shearings, what have you. Eighty-eight holes in our aircraft. Took a lump of steel to the machine-shop and they knocked up this little box for me. Engraved it too. – I've always kept it with me, Joe.'

You examined it in your hand. Polished steel. Didn't have the softness of silver. Strange how the fingers can tell the difference.

'Wasn't the same man afterwards, Joe. Once you go through the gate, it's not easy to get back to normal. I had no respect for civilian life. *Bugger the rules* was my attitude. How can you respect the rules when you've spent two years killing, like a fox among hens, and got away with it? "Bugger the rules. I shall do what the hell I please!" was what I said to myself.' Johnny Mitchell took a pinch of snuff from the Krupps box, passed it to you with his finger. His eyes were blue as a winter sea, off hot Tenerife.

'In civilian life, people make mountains out of molehills. Do you understand me, Joe?' The snuff smouldered behind your face. Of course you understood, you knew this as well as you knew the world. 'For instance, an acquaintance might say to me, "Johnny, I am getting a pain in the arse from so-and-so, and I just do not know what can I do about it." I knew what to do, Joe. It was easy. Follow so-and-so down an alley, or a country lane, and break his face. Fill a tweed sock with half-crowns and break his face. – Then collect from your acquaintance.'

The wind rustled the trees in the quiet road and the palm in the garden next to W8. 'I didn't make mountains out of molehills, Joe. Where others saw a vast bloody barrier, I saw the way clear. – You understand me, Joe.

'I was in business too. Lord, lost count of the businesses I've had. But always my own boss. That was cardinal. Sold cosmetics, wedding dresses, tools, parts.' Johnny Mitchell remembered. 'Had a garage, Great North Road. Couple of hotels, one in Devon, one in Brum…I've sold eggs – had a stall up in Kilburn. People wanted fresh eggs after the war. The housewife'd do anything for a fresh egg. If she was skint, we'd come to an agreement. Do you follow me, Joe?' Johnny Mitchell winked. 'Don't insist on rules, you see, and don't fix prices! Don't say *this is my way and my only way of operating*! Don't maintain with your hand on your heart that there are certain lines you will never cross. – That's been my way, Joe. That's the way you gather the world up in your arms. That is how you make money; that is how you enjoy yourself. – Do you know what I mean, buck?' You knew what he meant.

'Ah the things I've seen, Joe. The things I've known…' Johnny Mitchell was tired. He'd finished his Campari, and was looking across the road at number thirty-nine. You pay now, Joe. You will come again.

Next day, however, you were in Victoria till after six with a South African; you were worried he'd have vanished by the time you arrived. It was as hot as hell on the tube. The big clock at Triangle Sidings E&D said it was six thirty-five. He'd be sure to leave before seven. Why was there a clock that size underground, in the half-light between Gloucester Road and High Street Kensington? Ha! For to tell you the time, Joe. That was why.

He was wearing dark glasses, strange on a man of his age, and drinking a pint of dark liquid, though W8 wasn't the sort of bar that serves pints. He said, 'Ah, Joe!', in a voice weak and merry, as if he'd just been laughing more than was good for the lungs. You had the traditional bottle of beer. The evening temperature was still in the thirties. 'Joe,' he leaned towards you, 'what did you think the time you walked past and saluted?' You didn't answer.

'Thought I was ancient, didn't you, Joe? – Thought I was ancient, and you were modern! And you were right! – But Joe,' he looked blind, hilarious, 'you should have seen what we were like in the old days! Had fun in the old days, Joe! Permissive society put an end to that. We were at it like devils! By God you should have seen us!' He leaned towards you: 'It's like a religion nowadays. Where's the fun in religion, Joe? Tell me that!'

You considered your ways and all the people you fucked. He might be right.

'Hildy was the best, Joe. Forty years of marriage. We saw eye to eye on absolutely everything. She was the *best!* We took a Caribbean cruise for our honeymoon. I flew twenty-five of our friends out to Barbados for a special party. Unforgettable. They're still talking about it, Joe. I swear to you!' Johnny Mitchell softly karate-chopped the table and smiled behind his dark glasses. 'She was a big blonde, Joe.' Johnny Mitchell shaped Hildy in the hot air. Bubbles seethed in his black drink. 'She knew what I liked, and I knew what she wanted. Rescued her from a bad marriage, Joe. Both knew we were in it for life. Till death do us part.' Johnny Mitchell raised his dark glasses. His eyes were wet.

'She used to say to me, "Doesn't matter if you have other girlfriends, Johnny. You have too much spunk in you for one woman, darling! Too much spunk, you old devil!"' Johnny Mitchell lowered his dark glasses again and began to sing slowly:

'Where you've gone darling
I shall soon follow
To heaven or hell
I shall soon follow

Life is still sweet
But not sweet enough
So where you've gone I shall soon follow.'

You should have clapped, Joe – or done something, but you just sat there as the song finished, so he must speak again: 'I'll be going soon, Joe. Won't be long now. But what I've been and done is as permanent as mountains. Ain't that so, Joe?' You nodded your head and touched his cold hand. 'Here, Joe.' He pushed the steel box engraved Krupps XIXth towards you, with as much effort as if its mass had multiplied wildly. 'I have no further use for it. Put it in your pocket.'

Johnny Mitchell crossed the road to number thirty-nine and went through the gate, then you walked away. The snuff box lay hard against your heart, as you compared yourself with all you had learned.

Like Pepper
Judy Piesse

The pepper grinder is calling to her from the shelf. She doesn't know why it would do such a thing – it's not as if she's that partial to pepper; more of a sweet tooth, if anything. But there it is. The red, shiny pepper pot, with a silver top marked 'P'. She thinks of how it would look on her table, a centrepiece in the middle of steaming dishes, and before she's had a chance to think, before she can stop, her fingers spring forward. She lifts it up her coat sleeve, enticing it to nestle.

It's up there, bulging discretely, and she's walking down the aisle, steadily, as if doing a drink-drive test in a room full of policemen. The lights are very white, and they're playing jazz all of a sudden, and she can hardly bear it, this trying not to rush. She catches sight of herself in the mirror, walking past rows of pans: red-cheeked, eyes shining, grey-brown hair dishevelled.

'Can I help you?' a woman says. She has lunged out from nowhere; a short woman with dark brown eyes, and a quizzical look that must be part of her job.

'No thanks. I'm fine.'

'Are you looking for anything in particular?'

'Just window shopping,' she says. Pan-faced and empty; she knows they won't notice. 'Don't need any help. I'm fine.'

Lynne wonders if people can guess through the leather, inside the squat handbag where the red is now gleaming. She's walking down the high street, past Top Shop and Next, where the kids gather to flirt and ride skateboards. The girls dress up in mini-skirts and black eye make-up and have jaunty, angular hairstyles. Things she couldn't have afforded at their age. She sits down on the steps outside the shops, and feels the outline of her handbag, her breath calming down as she strokes its new weight. A group of teenagers light up in a circle, absorbed in each other and veiled by white smoke.

Mary's birthday tea tonight, mustn't forget anything. Sellotape and wrapping paper, and Perrier, because Mary doesn't like wine, and gravy for the beef that she can't eat anyway, because it sticks in her throat and makes it dry.

She can see them now, how it will be: Mary with her flat pills lined up in neat tracks; Kenny, next to his mother, bald spot gleaming; Lynne, squeezed round the back of the table, tucked in beneath the window on the other side.

Kenny is doing the dishes left over from lunch when Lynne gets home. He is bent over the basin in yellow marigolds, patiently washing. He does more around the house these days; she wishes he wouldn't. She can smell Mary's presence: windows closed too long, boiled, salted veg. The house has smelt this way for over six months, since Mary moved in, and Ben left home.

'Your mum okay?' She rubs her head.

'Hmm.' Voice lukewarm and nasal. 'Big night tonight!' He turns round to face her. 'Get anything nice?'

Lynne looks at the dishes on the draining board, soap suds still bursting.

He wipes the taps with a damp cloth. 'Mum's gone upstairs.'

As Lynne goes up to wrap Mary's present – a pair of slippers and a box of chocolates to be presented after dinner – she can hear the snores coming from her room. Loud and coarse from such a tiny body, amplified by the corridor which drags the sounds out like a lung.

She spreads out the paper on the bedroom carpet and puts the chocolates in the centre. She cuts off four pieces of Sellotape and tacks them to the bottom of the dresser, mindful of fluff and errant hairs. She looks at the gilt box lying before her, at the mountains and sky of an Alpine scene. In the years before The Poplars, she'd got herself treats like these. Six rows of plump truffles, fat and willing. Garnished with white chocolate shavings, or dark coffee dust. She'd sit and eat them by the telly, all lonely and special. Comforting and squidgy, they were something of her own.

She wraps up the chocolates, and thinks of Mary. Doll-like, but brittle, in Ben's old bed. Silk hair unsheathed, mouth pink at the corners. Fierce snores still flushing the length of the corridor. Faraway, holding back, then bursting up close.

Later, as she lays the table, smoothes down the first tablecloth in case of spillages, and then the second embroidered one on top, Lynne thinks of Ben. She has searched her mind, and found no satisfactory answer as to why he had to move so far away. He's out there, on his own, and she doesn't know what he's doing. She knows which city of course, but none of the details: where he gets his shopping, what he eats for dinner, how often he washes his clothes.

She can picture only the tall, dingy house which she visited after Christmas, snow still lining the gutters; the long, grey lines of a January coast. The stained beige settee and chipped blue dishes. If she'd only had the nerve to offer to clean up.

The new girlfriend was there of course. Jayne. Short. Frizzy hair. Pretty heart-shaped face, and long eyelashes. Always polite. Made the tea, and set out coconut biscuits in a lucky horseshoe ring. Clever, too. She gave Lynne no reason to ever complain. They sat in the living room, talking about the furnishings. The three of them together. Measuring time.

'Don't you want to get yourself a better settee?' Lynne said, before she left. She couldn't help herself. 'If you're hard up, you know to ask.'

But Jayne had said, no, they were students after all. They hardly ever noticed. They didn't really mind.

She checked Ben over as he slumped on the broken springs to see that nothing could be missing, just as she had on that very first day. His nut brown hair, and crooked ears; the reassuring length of his legs and arms. All the best bits of his father, and none of the bad things: the too-pale eyes and russet skin. When he was born the nurse, who might have seen her in the papers, leaned in and whispered: 'You know Mrs Eldridge, you won't need nothing else.' Lynne can remember the nurse's sweet doughy smile and how her gold bracelet flashed, elementally bright.

On the doorstep they hugged and said goodbye. Lynne said: 'Keep up with your studies.' She could not be more precise. She tried to remain steady as she turned away, but she sensed her guts twitching, pulling her back. She felt a prickling on her cheeks and a dryness in her throat. She knew she wasn't supposed to feel like this: to want to clutch and howl and thirst.

She puts the pepper grinder in place, and pats the cloth where Mary sits. Embroidered windmills, their arms locked in motion, encircling flaxen-haired boys and girls.

Kenny is chewing his Yorkshire puddings as if they are made of rubber. He has small, neat peg teeth; too small for his lips, which are pink and full.

'Lovely,' he says.

The dining room is dominated by the table and three chairs, with a small, high window behind Lynne's head. The light beams onto the brown of her hair and turns it slippery, potato-skin pale.

She never has been sure about his mouth, not in all these years. She consoled herself in the early days, when they had to kiss. She thought to herself, at least he's tall. Mother-loved, stooped, big shy hands fumbling. 'We won't talk about it. That's done with now.'

'Are you okay with that?' Kenny asks Mary. Sometimes he cuts her food up into little pieces. He does it patiently, for as long as she needs.

Mary nods and carries on sawing. 'Just a little more salt, dear, if you don't mind.'

She points at the pepper grinder as Kenny does the shaking. 'Did you get that down the town?' Her voice is brisk and casual, just slightly too shrill.

Lynne buries her gaze into the softness of the tablecloth. The windmill arms and rosy girls.

'How much d'you pay for a thing like that?'

Lynne's head has started pounding. 'Just five pounds.'

'That's good, isn't it?' says Kenny. He sits back down, but the women ignore him. He starts blowing on his hands, as if he feels cold.

'Do them cheaper up the market, I'll bet. I'll bet they have them for under five pounds.' Mary mops her chin with a napkin, folds it neatly by her plate. 'You really want to shop around.'

'Now, you know what they say about women who shop too much,' Kenny starts, and he leans slightly forward, furrowing his eyebrows to indicate the joke. 'They say…'

Lynne hates it most when he tries to be funny, and she hates it when he sticks up for his mother. She grinds the pepper loudly: grate, grate, grate. It's hers, hers, and she doesn't bloody care what anyone says about it.

'Shouldn't have too much pepper on your food,' Mary says, the corners of her mouth red, her lips quite pale.

Disapproval has quickened in her with age; grown justified, brighter, as she has grown frailer. 'When I was on the farm, my granny used to say that too much pepper is bad for the lungs.' She points at her windpipe. 'Hot, you know.' She pauses, watchful. 'Doesn't twist properly. I'd take that back, if I were you.'

Lynne feels the tightness in her skull, as if her thoughts are being crushed. She slams down the grinder with a force the cloth can't hide. All at once she sees full stops. One launches into Mary's glass, and falls to its release: the Perrier's fizz, the lengthened pause, the open and shut of Mary's mouth – a Swiss clock cheated of its tick.

'Never mind, love,' Kenny says, looking at no one in particular. He bobs beneath the table for the pepper grinder, and comes up flushed and shiny.

Mary fishes at the peppercorn in her glass, unruffled. She refolds her napkin, to show she's used to such outbursts. 'I was only trying to say. You could get a nice matching porcelain pair from the market for under…five…pounds…' She annunciates each word, making sure she is heard.

She has lived, after all, her whole life in this town. She examines her daughter-in-law, just the same in the flesh. Glancing off to one side, all butter wouldn't melt, the whites of her under-eyes crescent and raised. She can see that look clearly, as if she'd cut out the photo and framed it on the telly – and she could have done worse. Shoplifter, son stealer, poor little Miss Innocent. Just like him to take her on, never saying a word.

'Strange that Ben hasn't rung yet…' she says, shifting the tone, tight-lipped.

'His gran's birthday,' Kenny says. 'You don't suppose he's forgot?'

Lynne crushes two stray peppercorns through a pool of spilt salt. Black on white; mind the little girl's face. She's listening carefully for what is still missing. Through the tight sounds of swallowing, the rhythm of knives. She wets her finger and dabs at the mixture. For a moment she pauses, then closes her mouth. The taste of the seasoning, grainy and hot.

Later, when Lynne is sitting in the living room with her quiet cup of tea getting cold she hears Mary and Kenny talking in the kitchen: lazy, comfortable, mother and son. She clutches a cushion, and closes her eyes. She thinks of Ben; his arms loose around her. His face in the doorway, smiling her off.

'Too big,' Mary is saying, not quiet enough, testing. 'Too big. You'll have to change them for the next size. I'll ask Lynne to take them to the shop and change them for me. Why does she always get them a size too big? Doesn't she think to check the fit?'

He hesitates for a moment; his needs as great. 'I don't know. You'd think she might.'

Pray For Me, Jimmy

Les Lloyd

No matter the timing you always catch Jimmy No Smokes in the aftermath of some devastating crisis or crushing personal defeat – flood, fire, sobriety, it's often like that with soaks, the real drinkers. They live in a permanent state of precarious unbalance, reeling from one hazy catastrophe to the next.

He earned his nickname around the town by apologetically sponging cigarettes and tobacco from unsuspecting strangers. He would swoop on a cigarette box left unattended on a bar room table with the speed and technique of a hunting owl.

The joke was that his favourite brands of smokes are the finest hand-rolled OP cigarettes. An abbreviation for other peoples'.

Personal bad luck follows him around like the scent of cheap and nasty aftershave. It swirls around him in an evanescent cloud and shows in his wounded animal eyes. The eyes of an old, ataxic dog being lifted onto the vet's examination table for the last time by the bawling owner.

Often stuck for words and unable to express himself Jimmy forces a half smile for punctuation while struggling to compute his next sentence. The fragile smile evaporates before it reaches those soulful eyes and he comes across as stoic. Reminiscent of a valiant terminal cancer patient giving you the thumbs up from his hospital bed.

He had been a permanent fixture around the estate's smoky dive bars, pool halls and council blocks for years. Originally from a well off family from the private houses he had spurned any deliberate hint of upward mobility after a passionate love affair with Jack Kerouac novels. He suddenly began chanting 'Integrity and personal freedom' as a mantra to his accountant father and refused his weekly allowance, plunging into his beat-inspired lifestyle, taking solace with the estate's teeming decadent low life. I think he found the whole retreatist thing romantic and decadent, and above all else, convenient.

He fitted in effortlessly.

Tall, sensitive and well read. You could always find him in some drug dealer's smoke-filled living room, heavy lidded in the corner, ploughing through an obscure science fiction paperback while the rest of the crowd bicker about mindless football results.

On the top landing, way down the blocks towards the garage off-licence, lived an old acquaintance of mine called Neil. Never did catch his surname. Worked the same circuit as myself on the soul-destroying clock-watching agency jobs around the town's factories and sprawling industrial estates. You can't get a job in this town without some extortion racket employment service skimming your wages…packing fruit cocktails into boxes, squeezing bottles of contact lens solution, washing ready-made salads in a rusty metal drum. All manner of repetitive tasks broken down into step by step idiocy.

This allows the powers that be to dismiss employees on a whim and have another drone supplied pronto. Only five minutes on the job training required. Full instructions along the lines of:

'Okay, as the jars of mustard roll along the conveyor you stand here and slip one of these sleeves over the lid. Understand?'

At night you bolt upright in your sleep screaming in sweaty knotted sheets 'They're piling up! They're piling up! Turn the fucker off! It's running too fast!'

Neil was one of the desperate I encountered at every turn in each dirty, grimy factory. Six a.m., stood swaying in a dreary grey warehouse, waiting to be designated a cacophonous production line for the day. One day he leans over to me and, under the din of rattling bottles and clanging metal, he whispers:

'I'm putting out amphetamine if you know anyone who wants any...good strong base speed...an eighth for a tenner....real rocket fuel whiz. Here's my address and number.' It was two minute's walk along the landing from my flat. I didn't even have to step out into the rain.

The first time I walked into his flat it was like a high school reunion. The motley crew sat around smoking and snorting into the Sunday dawn were a cross section of my classmates and those in the same year from a rival catholic school. Deadbeats, time-wasters, drunks, and there's the ubiquitous Jimmy No Smokes squatting in the corner rifling the CD collection.

It took me a month or so to realise that Jimmy and his conjoined best buddy Kearney were in too deep. Sat grinding their teeth, garrulous and jabbering on about schooldays and teachers. I wasn't interested. Those things are best forgotten about.

Inseparable friends are like that, like being two bi-polar halves of the whole. Whenever one feels the need for a chemical heaven pick-me-up the other will just go along for the ride. They drag each other down that steep slippery slope with the very best of intentions.

Within a year they had both been sectioned for stints in the Booker Centre, the local residential mental health unit adjoining our skeleton-staffed hospital.

Kearney, it seems, got off lightly. Five consecutive sleepless nights and he started hearing sinister voices in his bathroom wall space, whispered threats and terrible accusations. All emanating from the wall above the bath where all that asbestos used to live.

The blocks that dominate our 1970s built, overspill hometown, are designed along the lines of prison block hives. Elongated and built lengthways with seemingly endless communal landings. Every door opening onto a mile-long deck, neighbours above, below and on either side. Virtually every open window and door throbbing with music. The wafer-thin walls let the slightest sound through. You can tell the neighbours moods by the music they are playing.

One speed binge too many, distraught and racing paranoid, Kearney decides it's do or die and rips the wall cavity to pieces in the early hours. Stood stark naked in his bath with torn bloody fingernails scraping the plasterboard to get at the voices conspiring against him.

Seven a.m. He comes crashing through the papier-mâché-like wall and staggers into the living room of the elderly couple next door.

Naked and wild-eyed he starts bellowing and lashing decorative ornaments and porcelain figurines at the walls.

Mr and Mrs Quiet Old Age, thirty-five years married and terrified, barricade themselves in the kitchen and call the police.

Five minutes later armed police drag a nude and delusional lunatic kicking and howling from the doorway out onto the landing. He doesn't go easy. The furious officers have to pry his white finger grip from the door jamb. The younger neighbours barely bat an eyelash. It's all in a day's entertainment. A death row cabaret. Once they realise the police are here for someone else it's party time. Groups quickly come spilling out from the doors all along the landing. Relief is in the air. Bottles and joints pass back and forth to fully enjoy the show.

As the blocks are home to so much of the town's proliferating criminal activity they draw dozens of emergency calls in any given twenty-four hour period. Upon receiving a 999 call the authorities invariably respond by dispatching a rapid response team and paramedic unit in that order. (It's a rolling joke that the local drug squad do not require or accept any offers of information, instead operating on a 'tombola' system of targeting drug raids. Raffle tickets in a hat. 'Flat number 225, today is your unlucky day.')

Kearney: Five months rehabilitation, three square meals a day, enough sedatives to drop a rhino.

First visit, Jimmy volunteers to take over the occupancy of Kearney's flat until he gets out.

'You can't leave the place empty, you know that. They'll have it stripped in an hour. I'll stop over until you come home. Look, the housing trust is sending a plasterer out on Tuesday. Don't worry about a thing. I'll have the place spick and span for you for when you are feeling better. Just take it one day at a time.' Exit Jimmy rubbing his hands with glee.

Within a week the place has an open door policy, every imaginable type of shady character and con artist streaming through the place. Desperadoes and charlatans every fucking one. The flat has the chaotic, desperate feel of a wartime train station.

Two weeks in and Jimmy gives up the losing battle. He can't stem the tide of maniacs and dipsos charging through the door. The place has become an established drop-in centre for the lost and hopeless. Moochers come swarming from far and wide, every dark corner of the estate. Not being the most assertive of men No Smokes takes the only sensible option and joins in the fun with breathtaking abandon. Non-stop, exhausting amphetamine abuse.

For beginners:

Carefully wrap a gram of the potent yellowing powder in a cigarette paper and chase it down with a mouthful of lager…twenty minutes later you are telling a complete stranger about your sexual dysfunction, self-esteem problems, and how it's still too painful to listen to Kurt's lyrics. A few pulse-racing hours later and the vertiginous ascent levels off, slows and recedes, a steep descent creeps in and you begin to descend into a nervous depression. BOOM! Another bomb and you are straight back up to the stars and moon. Five days later you can barely stand up straight, hunched over like an arthritic ninety-year-old. Zero energy, respiratory system running on oxygen fumes, legs of lead, head too heavy to support.

To shake off the fatigue you splash water on your face…the water runs a murky grey between your trembling fingers.

An amphetamine habit and loneliness make for desperate, tragic friendships.

Forged in drug users' dire need of company and the transient's need of a bed for the night, this town is full of circling vultures. On a sunny afternoon you can see the wheeling shadows on the concrete. Anyone passing is great company when you are racing into the horizon on speed, no matter their motives.

Jimmy took up with a local drunk called Eddie. Ten years his senior pushing forty-five.

Eddie sports an eye patch and the weather beaten

weariness of a derelict street wino. Skin sunburned the colour of copper from summers spent street drinking out in the open…high street benches and kids' parks, waking stretched out on abandoned kerbside couches. Because of this he has a deeply creased face with the texture of an old leather boot, a black can tan.

Squatting in Kearney's flat they quickly make a routine of eight a.m. beer runs along the bustling walkway to the off-licence. Back home and they idly while away the rainy days lazing around the sparsely furnished flat. A well worn patterned settee and mismatched armchair, the stuffing hanging out of the torn arms, overflowing ashtrays, no central heating, rickety dining table and chairs, a refrigerator full of cheap lager and mounds of yellowed street amphetamine on the sticky, coffee cup-ringed sepia tinted glass table.

They are waiting for the horse racing on Channel Five. Each drifting in their own bubble, lost in an alcoholic pocket of silence, the drunken time slips that you experience in a crowded Christmas bar. You suddenly realise that someone that you were with left an hour ago.

Jimmy is suddenly torn from this hazy, smoke-filled serenity when Eddie vaults electrified from the cocoon of his seat and starts screaming and bellowing:

'Jimmy! Jimmy! I'm going to die Jimmy! I'm dying Jimmy! I'm going! I can feel it! Pray for me, Jimmy!' and dives behind the couch cowering, wailing, thrashing like a hooked marlin.

Heartbeat rushing pleasantly through his ears and nicely intoxicated, Jimmy's slow to react.

'Listen' he says languidly raising himself from the warm, womb-like comfort of his armchair, heavy lids and room spin, 'what's, what's the problem?' he says swaying. He peeks over the back of the settee and sees his drinking partner curled into the foetal position, whimpering and shaking like a beaten dog. (Jimmy told me later: 'You would have thought he was being kicked to death.'). He reaches over to calm him.

'Eddie. Eddie! It will pass. It's just the fear, mate. It's just the fear! We all get it now and then. Just ride it out and relax.'

Eddie lashes out and will not be consoled, he's seeing demons, he thrashes around kicking furniture, pounding floorboards, jarring cold radiators. Jimmy quickly assesses the situation – the time, the screaming, the already exasperated neighbours constantly complaining to the housing trust about the drunken brawls and shouting at all hours. He fears an errant phone call and a rapid drug bust.

'OKAY! OKAY! I'LL GET SOMEONE! JUST KEEP QUIET AND CALM DOWN!' He runs out onto the landing and finds it completely deserted from one end to the other. He knocks frantically at doors. No one answers.

Hearing that sort of racket most neighbours will casually turn the TV volume up or down and plead ignorance.

In a blind panic Jimmy sprints along the decks, hammering on doors as he goes.

Finally, a confused, drunken pensioner suspiciously lets him into the hallway, points over to the phone and lets him call for an ambulance. His words come gushing out in a torrent. He has to repeat himself several times before the operator understands him. He dashes back. By now Eddie is pallid, terrified, he smells of ammonia, a steaming stain spreading on his crotch and he's howling 'Jimmy! Jimmy! Pray for me, Jimmy! Please just pray for me!'

The paramedics arrive in minutes. Appearing from the next entrance along, bored and disinterested, rolling a stretcher up on wheels along the landing. The two ambulance attendants have the demeanour of twitchy shoplifters' look-outs, nervous and furtive. The address alone hints at an overdose, suicide or domestic dispute.

Hysterical, Eddie is grappled down onto the gurney, strapped down and hauled clattering down the stairs.

'Pray for me, Jimmy!'

The uniforms hurl their patient into the back of the ambulance and slam the doors. The speed and force employed in this task remind Jimmy of an enraged pizza cook. Lazily climbing into the driver's seat a supercilious attendant tells Jimmy he'll have to make his own way to the hospital. A squeal of the tyres and they are gone. Red lights turning onto the main road.

Shaken from his stupor and slurring drunken bliss, Jimmy starts thinking clearly.

First things first. And with that he heads back down the landing to the flat and starts tidying around. Empties into the bulging bin bag, tabletops wiped clean, weed and powder stashed away in the gap behind the bathroom sink support column. 'Probably took a whitey,' he thinks to himself, 'Bad speed. Probably pigged out on it while I was out of the room this morning. Oh, well…that's what you get with bad karma.'

Two joints later he's cruising and enjoying his medications, languidly making his way up to the emergency room, stopping now and then to chat along the way.

'Yeah, old Eddie freaked out! Man, you should have seen him go! Anyhow, I'm just off up to the wards to see him. I'll catch you later.

The words 'Dead On Arrival' made the earth spin beneath his feet. The reception room wheeled around and lifted from the ground, he swayed to accommodate the gravity pull. A nurse asked him if he was okay. He didn't hear another word.

As he told me about it later his face contorted and twisted. 'Les, I just kept thinking, I can call on Kearney and tell him the news while I am here. I couldn't get it out of my head. It was all so matter of fact…As if that would make it all right…You know, straighten everything out.' His bottom lip quivered like an upset child's.

Jimmy never recovered from the trauma. He wanders around the estate's dive bars shell-shocked, staring at himself in the bar mirrors and bumming smokes and begging drinks from annoyed, sometimes belligerent strangers.

Once in a while some young buck sizes him up with near military strategic planning for an easy victory – six foot plus, heavy build, look good in front of the boys no doubt. These predatory little pack-dog bastards cultivate a string of pushovers like the manager of a glass-jawed heavyweight. Anything for a bad reputation. Problem is Jimmy hasn't got the spark in him to fight back, the light's gone out, his anger has drained out. He can barely lift the weight of his arms to block the blows raining down on him. I've heard people say he takes the beatings as a penance.

One balmy evening last summer we were sat outside our local dive bar, The Fiddlers Elbow. Shane and I are sat swaying drunk on the graffiti-engraved benches, watching car headlights swinging across the brick walls and dipping our hands into off-licence carrier bags to refill our empty pint glasses. Just then Jimmy comes mincing down the lane in that short, quick-stepped way of his, nose swollen twice the size, thick as a plank between his bruised eyes. He starts straight in on a tale of woe. Jonny Lung Damage, the local contraband tobacco baron who lives just across the road there won't give him credit. Indignant at the injustice and fighting back tears he tells us:

'He knows I'm good for it! He knows it! I don't understand him! I really don't! The times he's given me baccy on tick and I've paid him back! I tell ya, he's nothing but an out and out bastard!'

It looks like his world has come to an end. Shane can't abide the man, 'You would think no one else had problems the way he bellyaches' he says under his breath and turns away in disgust. He has that effect on some people. They turn away from him slowly as he approaches, as if he has drained all energy from them.

'Just looking at him makes me feel ten years older.'

Jimmy attempts to turn on the charm. He knows I'm a

sucker for a sob story. Starts flirting in his obvious, flaming camp way. Reaches over and ruffles my hair. Notices my rugby shirt: 'I forgot that you've got that proud Welsh heritage thing going on.'

'Here we go.' You can hear Shane and the boys sigh in exasperation. He kicks me under the table and says sharply: 'DON'T!'

Five pints later: I'm broke and we are alone on the bench, Jimmy and I.

The estate is pitch dark and the night has the odd, nightmarish feeling you experience when you are stranded a long way from home. Anything can happen. It's closing time. The pub is letting out and we sit there in the neon glow of the opening and closing door. Taxis coming and going. Drunken old bingo winners ambling past and zigzagging up the path towards the late night fast-food joint up in the centre. Slurring couples bellowing effusive farewells up and down the road. Midnight goodbye kisses.

A few moments of eerie silence and Jimmy turns to me with his usual frown and says:

'Who's going to pray for me, Les? Do you think it's going to be you?'

Author Biographies

M Y Alam has several short stories published, two novels and has edited a collection of crime writing. In 2007 he edited *Made in Bradford*, a highly acclaimed anthology of conversations with young British Pakistani men. He is also a researcher and teacher at the University of Bradford working in the Department of Social Sciences and Humanities.

Alexis Clements is a 2006/2007 fellow of the Dramatists Guild of America and recipient of a Puffin Foundation Artist Grant for prose work. Clements' plays have been produced in both the UK and the US and her short stories have appeared in a handful of publications, including Route's *Ideas Above Our Station*. She has also written for such magazines as *Nature*, *Aesthetica*, and *Travel New England*. For more information visit www.alexisclements.com

Anthony Cropper has published two novels and has co-edited three collections of short stories. In 2005 he won the BBC Alfred Bradley Award for Radio Drama and subsequently wrote for Radio 4. He has worked on numerous projects, including the site specific installation, *Wanderlust*, a collaboration with Talking Birds.

Carla Gericke was born in South Africa, raised by diplomats, and has lived and travelled all over the world. She moved to America in 1995 after winning the green card lottery. Carla is a matriculating candidate in the MFA Creative Writing programme at The City College of New York, where she also teaches. She is the recipient of various awards and was honoured in 2007 with fellowships from Larry McMurtry and the A Room of Her Own Foundation. Her work has appeared in anthologies and in *ep;phany*, *Inkwell*, *Pindeldyboz*, *Route*, *Word Riot*, and elsewhere. Carla lives with her husband in Chinatown, New York City, where she is completing her first novel.

Pippa Griffin discovered the joy of the short on the long commute between Bedford and London, before moving to the capital fourteen years ago. She juggles her love of reading and writing short stories with freelance work. Any spare time finds her tinkling the ivories, attempting the tango and horse riding – all of which keep her osteopath in regular employment. Currently scribbling her way through an MA in creative writing at Birkbeck, University of London, this is her first published story.

Sophie Hannah is a bestselling poet and novelist. Her psychological thrillers *Little Face* and *Hurting Distance* have sold more than 150,000 copies in the UK, have been sold all over the world and are currently being made for television. Her latest poetry book, *Pessimism for Beginners*, is published by

Carcanet Press and was shortlisted for the 2007 TS Eliot Prize. Sophie lives in West Yorkshire with her husband and two children.

Les Lloyd was born in Liverpool and grew up in Runcorn. He currently works in a hotel and recently scrapped eighteen months of research into a novel based on a haunted hotel after seeing the movie version of Stephen King's *The Shining*.

Michael Nath has published stories and novel extracts in *Wonderwall* (Route16), *Ideas Above Our Station* (Route18), *Critical Quarterly*, *Stand*, *Billy Liar* and *Main Street Journal*. Michael has also written two novels and is close to completing a third (*La Rochelle*). He is a lecturer in English at the University of Westminster.

Dave Pescod studied visual arts and began writing jokes for radio and television. More recently after completing a Royal Literary Fund Mentor scheme he started writing prose. He has had stories published in magazines, broadcast on Radio 4 and is currently completing his first collection of stories.

Jude Piesse was born in 1979. She studied English at the University of Leeds and Creative Writing at the University of East Anglia. She has worked as a local newspaper reporter, an arts administrator, a library assistant, and an Open University tutor. She currently lives in Bristol.

Wayne Price was born in south Wales and now lives and works in Aberdeen. He has published short stories and poetry in a number of anthologies and literary journals in the UK, Ireland and America including *Stand, Poetry Wales, Passages, New Writing Scotland, Shorts: The Macallan Anthology* and *Carve*. He was a runner-up in the 2005 Bridport Short Story Prize, the 2007 Bridport Poetry Prize and the 2007 Fish Publishing Short Story Prize. He teaches literature and creative writing at the University of Aberdeen.

Paula Rawsthorne's tale 'The Sermon On The Mount' was a winner of the BBC Get Writing competition and was read by Bill Nighy on Radio 4. She has written a play for children's theatre and performances for a Notts heritage festival. Her story 'In Attendance' was published in *Ideas Above Our Station* (Route 18). Paula lives in Nottingham with Stan, Archie, Sadie and David.

Other Titles You May Enjoy

Ideas Above Our Station (Route 18)

ISBN: 978-1-901927-28-3

Someone is waiting for a train, or it could be a bus or an aeroplane. They are alone. For company, in their coat pocket they are carrying a book of stories. They sit down and take out the book. It falls open on the first page of a new story. What would be the perfect read for them to find there?

Route Compendium (Route 17)

ISBN: 978-1-901927-26-9

A festival of contemporary stories that brings together the first wave of Route's pioneering byteback books. Includes five original collections of contemporary fiction featuring: a showcase of bright young talent; the decorator's tale; stories of love and the trouble it can bring; modern folk tales and a collection of misfits which includes the most audacious car chase short story that you will probably ever read.

Wonderwall (Route 16)

ISBN: 978-1-901927-24-5

This title focuses on the people that matter most in our life; those close at hand – the family member, the friend, the colleague, the passer-by. These stories underline the uniqueness of our own existence, and emphasise that despite our world of instant global communication, it is the real people in our lives who affect us the most.

Comment on Route Series Titles

'Books that are making critics, and readers, sit up and take notice.' – **Yorkshire Post**

'The most interesting and vibrant publishing house around today.' – **Nottingham Evening Post**

'Route has arrived at a format which could almost be described as a northern *Granta*. For any broad-minded soul that cares to check it out, it remains hard evidence of a valid literary sensibility beyond London.' – **Artscene**

'Gleaned from the length and breadth of the UK, these stories do not disappoint. There is a grittiness to these tales, variously dealing in love, and fading or faded dreams and a commendable lack of adornment and sentimentality.' – **The Glasgow Herald**

'The sharpest, on the button writing you'll read all year. Route could soon start taking on a Samizdat level of importance as it quietly ushers in the beginnings of a much needed literary renaissance.' – **The Big Issue**

'Punchy, pithy and darkly humorous.' – **Liverpool Daily Post**

'A bit like going to a party and meeting one fascinating person after another.' – **Leeds Guide**

'Some of the best stories I have ever read.' – **BBCi**

'These stories drop you right into what's going on behind the curtains and in the alleys of your own neighbourhood.' – **Bradford Telegraph and Argus**

'The eclectic, the humorous, the heartbreaking, the psychological, the fear and angst are all here in a collection that not only embodies the city but occupies the very soul of the urban landscape.' – **Inc Writers**

The Route Series

Route publishes a regular series of titles
for which it offers an annual subscription.

Bonne Route (Route 19) is a title in the Route Series.

For details of the current subscription scheme
and complete book list please visit:

www.route-online.com